DESERT

The stage line was the only link between east and west, but for months now it had been under attack. The stages had been held up, riders shot down and passengers robbed. To try to stop the outlaws was suicide. That is what they told the man who rode into town one day and asked for the job. Soon he became their only hope as the renegades tried to stop the stage at one of the way stations, trapping the riders and passengers. There was no means of escape, and all about them lay hostile plains and impassable mountains . . .

E. F. GRANGER

DESERT SIEGE

Complete and Unabridged

LINFORD
Leicester

First hardcover edition published in
Great Britain in 2003
by arrangement with
Robert Hale Limited, London

Originally published in paperback as
Gun Range by Chuck Adams

First Linford Edition
published 2004
by arrangement with
Robert Hale Limited, London

British Library CIP Data

Granger, E. F.
    Desert siege.—Large print ed.—
Linford western library
1. Western stories
2. Large type books
I. Title II. Adams, Chuck. Gun range
813.5′4 [F]

ISBN 1–84395–475–3

Published by
F. A. Thorpe (Publishing)
Anstey, Leicestershire

Set by Words & Graphics Ltd.
Anstey, Leicestershire
Printed and bound in Great Britain by
T. J. International Ltd., Padstow, Cornwall

This book is printed on acid-free paper

The moral right of the author has been asserted

All characters in this book are fictional and any
resemblance to persons, living or dead
is purely coincidental

1

The Lone Rider

Snorting and puffing laboriously, the narrow gauge train pulled into Red Rock, the locomotive sending a plume of black smoke high into the still, hot air of early afternoon. From the rear of the last coach, a tall man stepped down on to the platform, carrying the small bag in his right hand. The heat of the afternoon struck quick and deep and he stood for a moment, rubbing the sweat from his forehead as he paused, staring about him, eyeing the other passengers who alighted from the train. A couple of sharp-faced men had stepped down and further along the train, several miners had climbed down, their bundles over their shoulders. The tall man moved along the platform as the train began to move out again with much hissing of steam and clanking of wheels. He had a lean face, the brows drawn straight over the clear, grey eyes; the look of a man who did not smile often.

The two well-dressed men passed him and moved out into the dusty street; evidently gamblers, come to make their pickings here. Opposite the station house, stood the stage depot and even as the other moved out of the building, a stage came rattling around the corner in a cloud of dust, kicked up by the pounding hoofs of the four horses in the traces. It slewed to a halt in front of the depot and the bearded oldster on the driver's seat tossed down the reins and clambered down into the street, paused for a moment to glance about him, then pulled the bottle of liquor from his hip pocket and took a quick swallow, before stamping up on to the boardwalk and into the depot.

Going in on the other's heels, the tall stranger went over to the register desk that stood by the far wall. The desk clerk glanced up at him, then lifted his brows slightly.

Pulling out a wad of bills, the other asked: 'What's the fare to Sherman City?'

'You figgerin' on goin' through to Sherman City by the stage?' There was a note of incredulity in the clerk's voice, but it was quickly hidden. 'You must be a stranger in this part of the territory.'

'Just got in on the rattler from the Junction,' nodded the other. 'But I can't see where that makes any difference.'

'You could've gone on into Sherman City by the railroad, mister.'

'Mebbe so. But I prefer to go the rest of the way by the stage. That is, if it's OK by you and the stage line.'

The clerk shrugged his thin, sloping shoulders. 'It's OK by me, mister, if that's the way you want it. The fare's fifteen dollars and that's the stage out yonder. It'll leave in ten minutes.' He took the money that the other handed to him, pulled the ledger on the desk towards him and picked up the pen from its wooden holder. 'I'll have to have your name, mister. Just for the company records, you understand.'

'Mannix — Cal Mannix.'

The other wrote the name slowly in the book, then closed it and slid it back into its original place. His eyes narrowed a little as his gaze ran up and down Cal's body. 'I notice you ain't carryin' any guns, mister,' he said slowly, rubbing his chin thoughtfully. 'That could be a mistake, especially if you take this stage into Sherman City.'

'Can't say I've ever found it necessary to tote guns around,' muttered the other. He bent to pick up the small bag. 'You got any objections if I ride up with the driver?'

'I ain't got none,' grunted the clerk. 'Reckon that if it's OK with Clem, then it's OK with me. But you'd better ask him first. He's an ornery old cuss at the best of times, but lately, he's been even worse. This is likely to be one of his last drives for the stage line.'

Cal considered the other narrowly for

a moment. 'Any reason for that?' he inquired. 'I reckon I noticed him come in just in front of me. Gettin' on in years, mebbe, but I'd say there was still a few more years of driving in him.'

'Could be. But there's talk that the stage line won't be operatin' through to Sherman City much longer. Surprises me that it hasn't closed already.'

Cal pushed back his hat and looked up at the other. 'Mister, I don't understand this. Reckon there's somethin' I ought to know before I trust myself to that stage.'

The clerk showed a flash of his white-toothed smile. But it was an uneasy smile that did not touch his eyes, merely twitched the edges of his mouth. 'I guess you've got a right to know what's been happenin' around these parts in the past few months, mister, seein' as how you're determined to ride that stage into Sherman City. It's been held up more times than I can remember. The outlaws took the strongbox on six occasions and three of their best drivers have been shot down makin' the trip. Nobody wants to travel by stage now. Can't say I blame 'em. Wouldn't like to take the chance myself. Not with those killers along the desert trail. That's why I figger it's wisest to carry a gun. No tellin' when you'll be needing it.'

'I reckon there'll be a rifle up with the driver,' grunted Cal. He picked up his bag and walked towards the door, turning as he reached it and said, over his shoulder: 'Thanks for the warnin' anyway, mister. I'll take good heed of it.'

Outside, the heat struck him forcibly. In the depot, he had not realized how cool the building was, but there was a huge cottonwood facing the building and he walked over and stood in its shade. At the end of the long, narrow street, the town lay open to the desert. The gleaming rails of the railroad ran alongside the trail for perhaps half a mile before they veered off to the south, running together until they seemed to meet in the sun-hazed distance, where the flat horizon shimmered and shook as though it were something seen through dark water; a lost emptiness of sand and chaparral, hot and unpleasant. In the other direction lay the centre of the town. A handful of abodes that skirted the street; a couple of stores and one solitary saloon that stood back to back with the hotel. A singularly convenient arrangement, Cal thought idly, slitting his eyes against the refracted glare of the sunlight.

A late arrival came hurrying to the stage depot, went inside. A small, weasel-faced man with sharp blue eyes under dark brows and a thin line of moustache. He carried a large gladstone bag and the leather of his boots was polished to a high gloss. Five minutes later, the driver came out, followed by the clerk and another burly man who heaved the steel box up on to the back of the stage, then said something in a low undertone to the clerk who nodded quickly in Cal's direction. Slowly, Cal made his way forward, walking around the side of the stage as the weasel-faced man in the wide-brimmed hat came hurrying out, glanced almost furtively up and down the dusty street, then clambered inside the coach, slamming the door behind him.

Without speaking, Cal climbed up on to the seat beside where the driver would sit and sat watching the others with a curiously detached interest. For a moment, the oldster's whiskers bristled and his eyes narrowed under the bushy white brows as they drew together. Then he said testily: 'Who gave yuh leave to ride up there, mister?'

'Nobody, I guess,' answered Cal easily. Unabashed, he added: 'But I've ridden inside that train from the Junction for most of the day and I'd certainly appreciate a little air, especially on the ride across the desert yonder.'

'All yuh'll git there is a face full of dust and sand,' grunted the other tartly.

'But I reckon if yuh want to sit there, yuh may as well. If we do git hit by those critters in the hills between here and Sherman City, yuh'll be the first to get perforated.'

'Thanks,' Cal grinned thinly. Settling back against the woodwork of the coach, he watched as two other boxes and the rest of the luggage were hoisted on board, then the driver clambered up stiffly beside him, lifted the reins, holding them loosely in his fists. He wore guns, as did most of the folk in these parts, tied low, the handles and the leather of the holsters well worn and smooth.

'Better watch Clem once you hit the desert trail,' called the burly man harshly with a wide grin that showed his uneven teeth, stained with brown tobacco juice. 'He usually lets her rip and you'll be lucky if you get there in one piece, even if those danged outlaws don't decide to hit the stage again.'

'Outlaws!' grunted Clem thickly. He glared down at the speaker. 'I've driven this stage for close on thirty years, along this very trail, and I've never been held up once.'

The driver flicked the whip expertly across the backs of the horses and he uttered a shrill yell that sent them moving along the dusty street and out of town, the stage rattling in every seam and bolt. Turning past the railroad, they headed out through the chaparral and then into the desert, as the shacks and twin-storied buildings drifted away behind them. The sun had climbed high now and scorched the desert with its fiery, pitiless glare. It was not going to be a pleasant journey at all, reflected Cal as he tried to move his body into a more comfortable position on the seat. The wood was hard and ground into his back, but he guessed that inside the coach itself, with the outside woodwork getting hot to the touch, it would soon be like an oven, with scarcely a breath of air.

Two miles out of town, the trail suddenly twisted to the left and pitched sharply up the side of a long ridge. Here, the four horses really had to lean to it adding their own dust to that which was already in the air, the hard placing of their hoofs striking up metallic echoes from the rocky trailbed. At the crest of the ridge, the trail levelled off somewhat and Clem was able to give the horses their heads, until the coach began to career along the hard-packed ribbon of sun-baked dust which was called a trail, although as far as Cal could see it had nothing to merit the name. Here and there, the trail was littered with stones and each time they hit one of these, the coach would buck and sway dangerously, leaping crazily from the trail, the wooden wheels crunching down again with a thunderous crack that threatened to tear them loose from the axles.

The landscape around them was stark and arid, a stretching emptiness of flat glaring sand, rimmed in the far distance by an upthrusting line of red, sandstone bluff's. Bitter sage grew in clustered clumps, but as for the rest of the desert, there was nothing growing there but the occasional twisted cactus and a little greasewood.

'Why'd yuh reckon that fella in there joined us at Red Rock?' grunted Clem as he tugged a bottle of whiskey from his hip pocket and took a long swallow. 'Seems to me he's the kind of man who could've taken the train and travelled in comfort.'

Cal lifted his brows. 'Reckon he must have had a good reason for travellin' with us.' He leaned a little to one side and glanced down into the coach. The passenger was seated with his back to him, lolling in one corner, his mouth open a little under the thin moustache, his eyes closed. 'Whoever he is, he seems to be sleepin' well in spite of this goddarned heat.' He straightened, glanced back at the driver beside him. 'Does it always get so goddamned hot here?'

'Most times,' acknowledged the other. He took a second swig at the bottle, held it up and stared at the level of the liquid in it against the glaring light of the sun. Then he held it out to Cal. 'Like a drink to wash down the dust?' he asked.

Cal hesitated, then nodded at the other's friendly gesture. The liquor went down his throat and expanded in a cloud of hazy warmth inside him. He coughed a little then handed the bottle back. Time passed and as the hours slipped by, they slowly took the edge off the harsh sun. Cal became aware that the scenery around them was changing gradually. They had now left the sandy flats behind and the team was pulling up a long, rocky incline, surrounded by a jumbled maze of rocks.

'Goin' through the Canyons now,' grunted the driver harshly. 'The way station is on the other side. About fifteen miles.'

'How long will it take to get there?' Cal asked idly.

The other ruffled his side whiskers. 'All depends. Yuh heard what they was saying back in Red Rock. Stages have been held up along this stretch of country, but barrin' accidents like that, I figger we should get there by nightfall.'

'And Sherman City? How long before we get there?'

The oldster glanced up apprehensively at the sky, screwed up his thin lips behind the thick beard. 'Weather's holdin' up pretty good, I reckon. We should make it by nightfall tomorrow.'

'As far as that?' muttered Cal musingly. 'Reckon I'm not used to these long distances yet.'

'Yuh ain't from this part of the territory then?'

'Nope. I'm from back east. But I'd like to stay on around here if I can. It's all so open and — ' He broke off sharply. He had meant to say peaceful, but if the stories he had heard back in Red Rock were anything to go by, then this part of the frontier was still far from peaceful.

'Guess I know what yuh mean,'

grunted the other. He leaned forward and flicked the long whip over the straining backs of the horses. The coach rattled and bumped forward, canting to one side as it careered over the loose stones. At one point, they ran alongside a sheer drop into a deep canyon, the side of the trail falling away for close on a hundred feet before it reached the tumbled mess of boulders at the bottom. Cal hung on to the side of the driving seat as the stage swayed precariously close to the edge. The wheels slithered a little as they rounded the curve and a shower of loose stones went rattling off down the sheer slope.

At the end of this section of the trail, they entered the bluffs which Cal had noticed on the far skyline shortly after they had pulled out of Red Rock. It still seemed incredible that in the still, clear air he had been able to see them for such a tremendous distance. There was a wild and abandoned grandeur about this part of the trail which took him out of himself. The tall pinnacles of red sandstone lifted high into the sky, lonely and vast, their contours weathered by long geological ages of wind and sun. Towering on either side of the trail which narrowed at this point, they shut out the direct rays of the sun, although even in the shadows the air still held its tremendous heat. Uncanny spires of red and black polished lava stood out from the plain, running for almost half a mile before they broke through them, out into the open flatness of the desert once more.

Reaching into his pocket, Cal pulled out his tobacco pouch, rolled himself a smoke, then offered the pouch to the driver. The other shook his head in reply. 'Got little use for 'em myself,' he said thickly, 'use tobacco in my own way.' As he spoke, he pulled out a thick wad of black tobacco, bit off a sizeable hunk and commenced to chew it methodically, running it around his cheeks as he did so.

Cal lit the cigarette, drew the smoke down into his lungs. His mouth and throat were dry and parched and the smoke was not refreshing, tending to burn him rather than give the pleasure he usually got from a cigarette. But he continued to smoke it. By now, his body had grown used to the continual up and down motion of the ancient stage and he was able to ignore the bumps and bruises on his body.

'You got any idea why these outlaws should want to hold up the stage between Red Rock and Sherman City?' he asked quietly, glancing sideways at the other. 'Seems to me they'd get far better pickin's if they held up the main route stages instead of this one. Can't be much gold or valuables carried with this line.'

Clem screwed up his mouth under the bushy whiskers, contemplated the trail ahead of them for a long moment before replying. 'Can't say I've ever given it much thought,' he growled after a while. 'Reckon though you've got a point there. Come tuh think of it, you're right. They jest hold up the stage and take what they can git from any passengers.'

Musingly, Cal said: 'Could be that they're tryin' to put this particular stage line outa business for some reason. These things have been known to happen, especially when the railroad is also running a line from Red Rock through to Sherman City.'

'Say, you ain't suggestin' that the railroad is in on this, are yuh?'

'I didn't say that, but it's somethin' worth thinkin' about. If I was interested in this, I'd certainly try to find out what's at the back of it all. Could be that somebody wants this particular line stopped so that the railroad gets all the passengers and the freight.'

Clem pulled the thick bushy brows together into a hard line. 'If I figgered yuh was right,' he muttered, 'I'd go out and git those polecats myself.'

'You got an interest in the stage line then?' asked Cal without looking round.

'Sort of,' confessed the other.

'Reckon yuh don't know the set-up here, mister. This line was run by Chris Holmes. He started it more'n fifteen years ago when he first came to this part of the territory. His daughter Norma is runnin' it now.'

'A woman runnin' a line like this?' There was a note of astonishment in Cal's voice.

'Sure, an' why not?' demanded the oldster indignantly. He uttered a sharp yell to the straining horses, then sank back in his seat, hanging on to the reins with all of his strength as the powerful stallions leapt forward, threatening to tear them from his hands. 'I've known Norma Holmes since she was knee-high to a grasshopper. She takes after her Pa all right. When he died two years ago, there was nobody left to take it over. Nothin' else she could do.'

'And now it looks as though somebody is determined to close her up, is that it?'

'Could be.' The other spat a wad of tobacco on to the trail, coughed a little as the dust dragged up by the pounding hoofs of the horses entered his nostrils. Reaching for the whiskey bottle, he took another pull at it, held it out to Cal, then drank again, as the other declined. 'Funny they never try to hold up the stage when I'm drivin'. Reckon they know I'd make a fight of it. Not like those other yeller-livered coyotes who call themselves stage drivers.'

He continued to simmer indignantly as he drove, the knuckles of his skinny fingers standing out under the flesh as he gripped the reins more tightly than was absolutely necessary.

The sun went down in a violent red glow that covered the whole of the western horizon while they were still out in the middle of the desert. But the scarlet glow did not last long. Within minutes, the world had become a blue place of deep shadows and the heat of the day faded swiftly, to be replaced by a coolness that flowed against their faces as they continued north-west. The smell of the hills hit them a while later and Clem slowed the horses a little from their previous punishing pace.

'Nearly at the way station,' he said, breaking the silence that had existed between them for almost half an hour. 'Another fifteen minutes and we should be there, with plenty of hot grub waitin' fer us.' He grinned broadly. 'Still got a long haul in front of us tomorrow across the worst stretch of country.'

'That where these outlaws usually hit the stage?'

Clem glanced at him narrowly, then said sharply. 'Reckon so, but we won't be bothered by 'em. Once we reach Sherman City, I aim to have a little talk with Norma Holmes; I figger I can run this stage line without help from those drivers who walked out on us.'

'They told me back at Red Rock that you'd soon be out of a job, that the line is goin' to be closed anyway. Somethin' about the strongbox bein' taken on several occasions.'

Clem snorted in disgust. 'If yuh ask

me, those drivers handed the strong-boxes over to these critters without a fight. If they'd used the rifle here, they'd have given 'em somethin' to think about.' His glance strayed back to Cal. 'Yuh sure yuh feel safe wanderin' around the frontier with no guns, mister? Can sometimes be mighty unhealthy, yuh know.'

'Like I told the clerk back in Red Rock, I ain't found any real need to carry a gun. Besides, as you've pointed out, there's this Winchester here, just in case we are attacked.'

The other's beard fanned out over his check shirt and he seemed to bristle with indignation. 'Unless I'm mighty mistaken, I guess yuh'll soon find that yuh need a gun in these parts if yuh want tuh stay alive, mister.'

He turned his attention back to the team, heaving on the reins as he guided them around a sharp bend in the trail where it ran between two towering pillars of rock. By now, it was almost dark and the pinnacles loomed up in front of them almost without warning, so that it was obvious that Clem had ridden this trail more times than he cared to tell and knew every inch of the way, even in the dark.

The way station stood facing the trail, a long, low-roofed building standing at one end of a long corral. Pale yellow gleams of light showed in the two windows that fronted the trail as the team ground to a halt and the stage rattled itself to a standstill with a creaking of wood and springs. Beyond the station, the trail itself was a pale grey scar on the dark face of the desert, stretching away into the night. As he climbed down from the seat, Cal picked out the restless sounds of horses in the corral, guessed they would make up the fresh team that would take them out the next day at sun-up.

He followed the driver into the dining room at the front of the building. A short, lean-faced man in a white apron came out from behind the bar as they entered and walked over to them.

'Right on time, Clem,' he observed, 'no trouble on the way in, I hope.'

'Weren't expectin' none,' grunted Clem through his whiskers. He sniffed at the air, then nodded happily. 'You got the same grub as always, Orval?'

'Same as you always get,' nodded the other. He glanced round at Cal and the other passenger who had just entered. 'Bring your bags inside, friends. Reckon you'll get a bed apiece tonight. We usually have half a dozen folk or more on the stage on this trip, sometimes a woman or two among 'em. Then we're a mite crowded for sleepin' accommodation.'

Ten minutes later, they were seated at the long wooden table while the man in the white apron brought them a bowl of stew, followed by fried potatoes, sowberry, cheese and bread. There was hot black coffee too, served in white cups. Cal sipped the mouth-flaying brew slowly, feeling it go down his throat in a burning stream. The grub was well cooked in spite of the fact that the agent seemed to be alone there, and Cal ate until he was satisfied, then pushed the empty plate away, and thrust back his chair, getting to his feet. Rolling himself a smoke, he walked over to the open door and stood with his back and shoulders against the thick wooden post, staring off into the night. Somewhere in the near distance, he heard the yapping wail of a coyote and further off there was the sound of horse's hoofs pounding over the desert, heading away from them, the faint noise vanishing into the distance. Overhead, the stars were out in their thousands, brilliant and hard, so close that it seemed he had only to lift his hand to be able to touch them. The golden lamplight barely pierced the darkness that lay just beyond the door and he could only just pick out the shape of the coach where it stood a few yards away close to the fence of the corral. The horses, he guessed, had been taken away for the night.

Clem came over a little while later, weaving a trifle unsteadily from side to side, still clutching a whiskey bottle in his right hand. His beard showed palely against his features.

Glancing at the other, who seemed to have lapsed into a somewhat sullen mood, Cal drawled: 'What's wrong, Clem? You figure that we may get jumped tomorrow when we ride out?' He chuckled faintly as he spoke. 'Beats me why you don't quit this job while the goin's good, if it's gettin' as bad as this.'

'It ain't funny,' rasped the other thickly. He took a deep swig from the bottle. 'But there does happen to be gold in that strongbox and they might try somethin' tomorrow.' He looked troubled. 'It's one hell of a position when a gang of coyotes can hold up the stage whenever they feel like it and still ride clear away every goshdarned time. If it ain't stopped soon, then I reckon the stage line will have tuh quit.'

He searched for his tobacco, bit off a chew and ran it around the inside of his mouth reflectively. 'Reckon sooner or later, they'll git around to bringing some sorta law an' order to this territory, but it seems the sheriff can do nothin' to stop these holdups. Could be that he's in cahoots with 'em all.'

Cal nodded. That was so often the case out here, the sheriffs and marshals lining their pockets with money from the outlaw bands, just so that they were not too careful when it came to trying to hunt them down. So long as they and their posses made a show of riding out after the owlhoots, most of the townsfolk were satisfied. Only a handful would start to shout if there was nothing done to bring these men to justice and they could be quickly silenced by a gunshot in the back as they rode down some dark street or out on the trail where there were no witnesses. Like the other said, there would surely come a time when law and order prevailed in these parts, but that was not yet, and he had no way of telling when it was likely to be.

The old-timer's head came up suddenly. He had a sly humour on his face now, and a bright wisdom showing at the back of his beady eyes. He said quietly: 'Yuh know why I keep on ridin' the stage, even when these varmits are doin' their level best to stop every coach that goes through?'

'Suppose you tell me.'

'Reckon it's because I know old Chris Holmes from way back. An honest man, not like most of 'em in this neck of the woods. When he was shot down, I threw in my lot with his daughter and I don't aim to sit around and see her run out of the territory by these owlhoots.'

'They told me back in Red Rock that you'd lost a heap of riders, most of 'em killed, but some wounded. You can't run a stage line without riders, old-timer, and one man ain't any good to keep the stage movin'.'

'We'll keep it movin',' said the old

one with a touch of impatience. 'I can still handle a rifle if I have tuh and I ain't backin' down against these critters when it comes to a showdown.'

★   ★   ★

At sun-up the next morning, Cal pulled on a fresh shirt, washed and shaved himself near the window of the small room at the rear of the way station, then walked through into the dining room. The stage had been brought around to the front of the building and Clem was outside, supervising the hitching of the fresh team into the traces. He came inside, muttering a little behind his beard, as Cal seated himself at the long table and prepared to eat the breakfast that had been prepared for them. A few moments later, the other passenger came into the room. As before, his clothing was immaculate and he showed no sign of the long journey of the previous day.

'Good morning,' he nodded, pulling

up a chair and sitting down. His glance strayed to Clem. 'Do you think we'll be leaving on time, driver?'

'Guess so. Ain't nothin' to stop us,' grunted the other. He still seemed to be simmering inwardly at the apparent incompetence of the agent in getting the horses ready.

'Then we ought to arrive in Sherman City some time during the afternoon.'

'That's right,' Clem eyed him thought-fully for a long moment, then went on: 'Yuh in a hurry or somethin', mister?'

'Well . . . I do have an important engagement in Sherman City this evening,' affirmed the other. 'By the way, my name is Condor, Herbert Condor, attorney.'

'An attorney,' murmured Cal, inter-ested. He might have guessed it, he thought inwardly. The dress picked him out from most men who came to this part of the frontier. He might have passed, at a pinch, for a gambler, but now that he came to study him more closely, he saw that this could not possibly be the case. He had that studious look about him which marked him out as either a doctor or a lawyer.

'In that case, we'll do our best to accommodate yuh,' broke in Clem harshly. He tackled the food on the plate in front of him, eating ravenously. Cal wondered where the inevitable whiskey bottle was. When they were finished, the sun was already high in the heavens and the skyline shimmered with the rising heat. Outside, the horses twitched their tails nervously as the clouds of sand flies settled in swarms about them, biting and irritating. Cal brushed them away from his face as he made his way across the small courtyard to the waiting stage. Clem walked beside him, his beard fanning out around his face. He merely grunted when Cal said: 'Mind if I ride up top with you again, old-timer?'

The other seemed to have accepted him a little, he thought, as he climbed up, paused to swing the metal strongbox up into place as the agent held it up to him. There was plenty of weight in it, he decided, and if Clem was right, and it held gold, then it was likely that the outlaws would make some attempt to hold up the stage before they got within sight of Sherman City. He threw a quick glance at the Winchester thrust into its scabbard beside the seat and acting on impulse, pulled it out, the long barrel shining bluely in the strong sunlight, and checked that it was loaded. Satisfied, he thrust it back, feeling a mite easier in his mind. Clem hauled himself up beside him, clung on to the wooden hand brake for a moment in an attempt to steady himself, then lowered himself heavily into his seat.

'You got everythin' you need, Clem?' called the agent, glancing up and shading his eyes against the glaring sunlight that streamed across the flat face of the desert.

'Reckon so. All my passengers are on board and the strongbox is up here with me.'

'Better take it easy through Snake Pass,' warned the other, nodding. 'If those outlaws are goin' to hit you along this trail, that's the most likely place for an ambush.' His gaze flickered from Clem to Cal. 'Reckon you can handle that Winchester, mister, if they do come?'

'He figgers there ain't no need fer a man to carry a gun,' said Clem harshly, but there was no malice in his tone. 'Guess if we do run into trouble, he can hold the horses and I'll handle the rifle.' He cackled loudly, then leaned forward in his seat and the whip cracked with an explosive sound over the lead horses. The team shouldered against the leather as one and the stage shuddered, then rumbled out across the courtyard, through a small grove of trees, then between rising walls of rock until it was out in the desert once more and the solitary cluster of buildings of the way station had vanished from sight. Leaning back, Cal closed his eyes, shutting out some of the glare of the sunlight although it even forced its way through closed lids, shining redly into his brain. Dust rose and filtered into their nostrils as the sun climbed higher into the white mirror of the cloudless heavens.

'Goin' to git hotter soon,' Clem threw a swift glance upward, eyes narrowed to mere slits, the skin of his cheeks puckered a little. 'By around noon, it'll be hotter'n the hinges o' hell in these flats.'

'Ain't there any point in taking a trail around the eastern edge of the desert?' asked Cal quietly, nodding in the direction of the tree line that showed as a dark shadow on the far horizon.

'That'd put more'n thirty miles on to the trail,' grunted the other in reply, 'and when you're runnin' a stage line, yuh have tuh take the shortest route yuh can, or somebody else'll come along and take the line from yuh.'

'Anybody come into Sherman City and offered to buy the line from the Holmes girl?'

The old-timer pursed his lips behind

the bushy beard as he pondered on that for a moment before shaking his head. 'Ain't ever heard of anybody doin' that,' he muttered, taking a bite out of the stick of black tobacco. He thrust it back into his pocket. 'Yuh figger somebody might be after the line, hopin' to run it themselves?'

'Well, it makes some kind of sense, doesn't it?'

'Sure, sure.' Some curiosity showed momentarily on the driver's face. 'But if anybody has made her an offer, she's said nothin' to me about it and I reckon I'd be the first she'd confide in if she intended to sell out and move back east.'

He flicked the long, slender whip over the backs of the straining horses. Already, their flanks were lathered and sweat gleamed on their backs and shoulders as they hauled the stage over the shifting alkali of the desert. Now that they were well away from the bluffs there was dust and more dust. Unending flat miles in which nothing moved and nothing existed to relieve the deadly monotony. Thoroughbraces creaked as the wheels tried to bite into the soft, shifting dust where it was difficult for them to obtain a grip.

High noon came and went in a haze of dusty, intolerable heat. Cal felt the sweat form on his forehead, rolling down his face, mingling with the dust to form streaks of irritation along his cheeks. By early afternoon, they were rapidly approaching the far edge of the alkali flats and tall bluffs lifted from the horizon, reaching up into the clear, cloudless sky, breaking the flat monotony. Cal rubbed the sweat from his eyes, shaded them against the glare of the sun, and peered ahead, his mind alert for trouble. He remembered what the agent at the way station had said; that this was likely to be the place where any outlaws would try to hold up the stage. Sweeping the horizon ahead of them with a quick glance which took in everything, he noticed where the trail from the desert led up into the craggy hills that lifted in front of them. Rocks stood high on either side and the trail narrowed here so that the coach would just scrape through the pass and no more. Beyond it, he guessed the trail would then widen out, although the terrain would still be rocky, with stunted bushes and mesquite on either side, perhaps a few short stretches of timber.

'This Snake Pass?' he asked tersely.

Without turning, the driver nodded. His face showed no sign of apprehension.

'This is where the agent reckoned any hold up would happen.'

'That's right. But you ain't got no call to worry none. I've driven this stage along this trail more times than I care to remember, and I ain't seen hair nor hide of any outlaws.'

'That don't mean to say we won't bump into 'em today,' Cal told him firmly. 'Especially if they've somehow got wind of that gold we're carrying in the strongbox.'

'Now how in tarnation could they know that?' demanded the other a trifle testily.

'You'd be surprised how quickly word of such a thing as that can travel in country like this,' said Cal grimly. He let his glance wander from side to side as the narrow pass loomed up in front of them and the little warning bell at the back of his mind began to ring. It was a signal that he had learned from past experience never to ignore. A strange sixth sense that had saved his life on several occasions in the past.

The other's perplexity was so genuine and amusing that Cal amost laughed aloud at him. 'You find that strange?' he said quietly. 'I reckon that any outlaw band in these hills will know details of everythin' carried by every stage that passes through. If the law in Sherman City is workin' in cahoots with these outlaws, you can be sure that the same goes for the law in Red Rock. Somebody there will be passin' on

information, feeding these men shipment details for the local stageline.'

'Guess yuh might be right at that,'
agreed the other. He flicked the whip
once more, the crack sounded oddly
loud as the echoes rattled back from the
rocky walls on either side of them. They
made their way up the stony incline,
then rolled on with a creaking of
springs into the narrow pass. The rocks
closed in on both sides but Clem
guided the team so expertly that
although there were scant inches on
either side of the coach, it did not touch
at any point. Cal let his breath go in
short pinches as they edged their way
through, out into a more open portion
of the trail, the hoofs of the horses
rattling on the solid rock of the trail
with an oddly metallic sound.

Well, thought Cal inwardly, if there
were any outlaws in these hills, they
would certainly have seen or heard
them by now and would be lying in wait
for them somewhere along the trail. He
let his gaze flick from side to side,

probing ahead for any sign of trouble, but they had proceeded for more than a mile beyond the pass before trouble showed up and it came from behind them. The sudden burst of firing cut through the stillness like the lash of a whip and glancing back over his shoulder, Cal caught sight of the small band of men riding out of the hills, cutting down towards the trail behind them, spurring their mounts on in a cloud of dust that almost completely obscured the riders.

'Goshdarn it, yuh were right,' grunted Clem tightly. He leaned forward, yelled at the top of his voice, flicking the whip over the horses, urging them on at an even faster rate. They had almost reached the crest of the incline and fifteen seconds later, drove over the top. In front of them the trail dropped away at an alarming rate, but the other did not slow their pace; rather he urged more speed from the straining horses. The coach rattled and swayed perilously from side to side and glancing down, Cal caught a fragmentary glimpse of the other passenger, his face a pale grey, hanging grimly to his seat as the sideways motion of the coach threatened to hurl him to the floor.

A swift glance told him that in spite of their speed, the outlaws were slowly gaining on them. Their mounts would be fresh and they had far less weight to haul.

'They're gainin' on us,' he shouted, raising his voice to make himself heard above the rattling of the coach.

'They're runnin' as fast as they'll go,' called the other. 'Hang on to your seat. It gets tricky down here.'

Dust rose up in an enveloping cloud as they raced around a sharp bend in the trail. The wheels rattled and swayed, jolting as they hit the rocks which littered the ground. At any moment, Cal expecting the stage to over-turn and spill them down the side of the treacherous slope, but somehow, they held to the trail. Behind them, the outlaws thundered along the narrow, winding trail. A flurry of shots bucketed out and Cal heard the vicious hum of lead as it flailed the air close to his head. Bending forward, he reached for the long-barrelled Winchester, pulling it smoothly from its scabbard.

2

Mesa Shoot-out

'Yuh sure yuh know how to handle that rifle?' grunted Clem harshly, glancing at him out of the corner of his eye.

Grimly, Cal said: 'I reckon I might be able to drop some of those buzzards out of their saddles.' He twisted around in his seat, resting his elbows on the roof of the swaying stage, squinting along the sights of the Winchester. Another shot droned past his head, hummed into the distance over the backs of the leaping horses. Knowing that his weapon had a greater range than the revolvers used by the outlaws, he drew a bead on the leading man, squeezed the trigger gently, felt the rifle jerk in his hands, then saw the man pitch sideways from his saddle, hit the dust trail heavily and roll over several times before lying still by the side of the trail, the riderless horse running on for several yards before it suddenly swerved and went plunging into the rocks. The other riders continued to spur their mounts, shooting as they came. Cal saw that there were four of them left now, that they were spreading out along both sides of the trail.

He sighted on a second man, sent a shot at him, saw the other jerk in the saddle as the slug hit him in the shoulder, but he still managed to retain his hold on the reins, pulling himself back upright in the saddle as his mount thundered on. But he had dropped his gun and was, to all intents, out of the chase. The rifle muzzle lifting a trifle, Cal aimed at one of the other men, but the shot went wide as the stage swerved suddenly and unexpectedly around a sharp bend in the trail and for a moment, the outlaws were lost to view.

'That's another two of 'em who won't bother us, but the others are still determined to catch up.'

'We can't go much faster, or we'll bust an axle and that'll be the end.'

'Just keep the stage on the trail,' shouted Cal above the rumbling of the wheels. He cast a quick glance along the trail that lay ahead of them. It still ran downgrade, but the steepness of the incline was not as great as before and now it stretched straight in front of them with no further bends and twists. One glance was all he had time for, then he swung his attention back to the riders on their tail, still coming up fast, half obscured by the dust cloud lifted by the pounding hoofs of their mounts.

The riders came closer. A bullet hit the roof of the stage and whined off in murderous ricochet. Clem uttered a sudden coughing moan, slumped forward in his seat. Swinging quickly, he grasped the oldster by the arm and hauled him back into an upright position. There was blood on the back of the other's shirt, a slowly spreading stain that soaked into the rough cloth. The reins were still held between his fingers, but he was slowly losing his hold on them. Cursing harshly under his breath, Cal said thickly: 'Can you hold on old-timer until I scare off these critters?'

'I reckon so.' The other spoke through harsh gasps of pain, but seemed to straighten himself up with an effort, tightening his grip. The horses continued to pound ahead, throwing up a cloud of smothering dust that assailed their nostrils and choked in their throats.

Cal took a swift bead, squeezed the trigger, holding the gun steady in his hands as the stage rocked and rolled from side to side. One of the horses reared and plunged as the shot struck home, pawing the air wildly, whinney-ing shrilly. The outlaw clung desperately to the reins, but a second later, the animal fell sideways and the man toppled out of the saddle, hitting the earth hard with a jolt that must have hammered all of the wind out of his lungs, leaving him lying on the ground beside the trail. The two remaining men pounded on after the running stage, firing as they rode, but most of their shots were going wild now. Swaying from side to side of the trail, the stage presented a more difficult target than it would have done had Clem been able to hold the horses in a straight path.

Cal emptied the rifle into the other men, switching his shots. For several minutes they continued their pursuit, then, as the hammer fell on an empty chamber, they suddenly broke off the pursuit and fled into the rocks.

Thrusting the empty rifle back into its scabbard, Cal leaned swiftly sideways and took the reins from the wounded driver's hands, easing him back into the seat. Hauling on them, he slowed the thunderous pace of the horses to a crawl and finally succeeded in halting the team at the end of the shallow incline under the spreading shade of a couple of cottonwood trees which grew at the side of the trail. Getting down, he reached up and helped the oldtimer down. The other's face was grey behind the beard and the stain on the back of his shirt had grown a little wider. Gently, Cal laid him down on the hard ground. The other passenger clambered out, his face white and shaken. He stared down at the injured man with his eyes popping for several moments, then glanced up as Cal said sharply.

'Quit lookin', mister, and help me with him. Can't you see that he's been badly hurt.'

'But those outlaws ... they might still come back now that we've stopped. Don't you think we ought to keep moving. Mebbe get him to a doctor?'

'We'll do that in good time,' said Cal through clenched teeth. 'I want to take a quick look at this wound of his. Then he'll ride in the coach with you and I'll drive on for the rest of the journey.'

He eased Clem over on to his stomach and carefully pulled the shirt away from his back. The blood was slowly congealing over the wound but he was able to make out the dark purple hole from which the blood still welled slowly. He gave a brief nod, half to himself. 'I reckon it's not quite as bad as it looks. The slug is still there, old-timer, but I figure a doctor ought to be able to probe for it and get it out for you. We'll get you into Sherman City pronto.'

'Those outlaws — ' whispered the lawyer hoarsely. 'Suppose they're still up yonder in the hills, watching us. Won't they ride down and attack us again now that they know he's been hit?'

Cal threw a swift glance up towards the tumbled mass of rocks and boulders that covered the edges of the trail along which they had just come. There was no sign of the outlaws but it was possible they were still there, keeping the stage in sight, perhaps waiting for a second chance to attack; but somehow, he didn't think so. They had suffered more casualties than they had bargained for when they had tried to ambush them

49

and he doubted if they would try any further attacks on them, for fear of getting a taste of the same medicine themselves.

'Help me get him into the coach,' he said finally.

'Sure, sure,' murmured the other. There was sweat on his face, running down in rivulets into his eyes and a lot of it was not due to the heat of the sun, thought Cal. But the other helped him willingly enough, heaving the old man's legs off the ground, backing with him up the steps of the stage, laying him carefully on the seat. Evidently the lawyer was anxious to be on his way and knew that this was the only way they would get out of this accursed place, by doing as Cal asked him.

'We were lucky to have you riding along with us,' remarked the lawyer as Cal shut the door and moved around the coach to climb up into the driver's seat. 'If you hadn't scared them off, we might all have been killed by now.'

'I doubt it,' grunted Cal thinly. 'They

weren't after us. They merely wanted that strongbox. The rest of us were just incidental. Better keep an eye on him during the rest of the journey. We've still plenty of distance to cover and I don't aim to dawdle the rest of the way. The sooner we get him to a doctor the better. Even if it isn't a serious wound in itself, he's losing a lot of blood.'

'Yuh sure yuh can handle the horses?' growled Clem from the opposite seat.

'Just you sit back and relax,' Cal told him. 'I'm takin' over now.'

Climbing up into the seat, he picked up the reins and the long, leather whip, cracked it over the necks of the lead horses, sat tall in the seat as the stage rolled on along the dry, dusty trail.

After a while, he pulled his bandana over his mouth and nostrils to keep out the dust, concentrating most of his attention on the rocks on either side of the trail, seeking out the first signs of anyone up there, watching the trail, knowing that he could rely on the horses to stay in the middle of the trail

51

without too much trouble. Dark purple shadows were beginning to lie on the low hills when the dark patch of green showed on the horizon ahead of them and after a few minutes, the patch of black that marked the position of Sherman City, lifted over the skyline and Cal was able to relax in his seat for the first time since he had left Red Rock. This, as far as he was concerned, was journey's end. This was where he intended to stay, if circumstances would let him. In the past, whenever he had attempted to settle down in a place such as this, something had happened to prevent it and now he had somehow grown cynical of everything.

Presently, they drove on to a broad trail which wound its way through lush green meadows on either side of them, past a slowly-flowing river that twisted its way through the countryside, and then over a wooden bridge which spanned a narrow creek and on into the main street of the town. Sherman City was a new, but already bustling town, just beginning to stretch a little at the seams. There were five hotels and more saloons than one could count, three banks and a half dozen livery stables, together with all of the usual stores. Dominating the centre of the town, where two broad streets met, was the Stanton Hotel, a three-storey building that stood head and shoulders above everything else in the town. It was apparently named after the founder of the town, Sherman Stanton, who had made a lucky, but rich, strike in the hills nearby and started the gold boom which had turned this place from a cluster of low, wooden shacks into a modern frontier town in a matter of ten years.

Cal drove the stage past the hotel, then halted it in front of the stage depot, jumped down as a man came hurrying out.

'What's happened to Clem?' asked the other harshly, with a faint note of alarm in his tone. 'Why isn't he drivin'?'

'We were attacked by a bunch of

outlaws,' Cal said quietly. 'They hit us just as we came through Snake Pass. They plugged Clem in the back. He's inside the coach. I figure he needs a doctor.'

'I'll get Doc Adams right away.' The other hurried off and a moment later, a small crowd gathered on the board-walk, staring into the coach. They were still there when the agent returned with a short, stout man bustling behind him, a man who carried a black bag that he set down on the boardwalk while Condor opened the door of the stage and stepped out.

While Doc Adams made his examination inside the coach, Cal rolled himself a smoke, lit it, his back resting against one of the wooden uprights. He let his glance run over the faces of the people in the small group nearby, watching them a little more closely than his attitude suggested. They had come here just out of curiosity, he decided finally, nothing more. Then he switched his glance a little as another man came hurrying along the board-walk, stepped down into the street. The faint light glinted on the badge he wore on his vest.

'Were you with the stage when this happened?' asked the other, turning to face Cal. His eyes were twin challenges.

'That's right,' Cal made a brief gesture in the direction of Condor. 'We were the only passengers from Red Rock. The name's Mannix.'

The sheriff's brows went up a shade. 'You here on business, Mister Mannix?'

'Not exactly. I hope to settle here. If the town suits me, then I'm sure I will.'

'I see.' The other nodded. He turned his glance back to Condor, where the other bent over the wounded driver, 'What about him? Do you know anythin' about him at all?'

'Only that he's an attorney and it was important that he should get into Sherman City tonight. His name's Condor.'

'Did either of you get a good look at any of the outlaws?'

'Not a chance. They were too far away. But if you care to ride back along the trail you might find a couple of them still stretched out where we left 'em.'

'You killed two of 'em?' This time there was a definite note of surprise in the lawman's tone.

'That's right. Only way we could fight 'em off. That was when the driver was hit in the back.'

The sheriff's smile was tight and hard, did not touch his eyes. 'That ain't goin' to stop 'em,' he said quietly. 'This is a funny business. Somebody's tryin' to ruin this stage-line.'

'Have you tried gettin' a posse together and ridin' out into the hills around Snake Pass?' enquired Cal.

The sheriff nodded. 'I've done that on more than one occasion, Mannix. I've even baited a trap for 'em, used a dummy strongbox with the stage, passed word along that it was bein' carried and then rode the stage myself with half a dozen of my men, ready for trouble, but they didn't bite.'

'You mean that somehow they got word about the trap?'

The other's eyes narrowed just a shade, then he nodded. 'That's it, I guess. Somebody is tippin' them off, either here or in Red Rock. They seem to know everythin' that travels on that stage, when it's safe to attack and when it ain't. Nothin' we do seems to catch them.'

Cal remembered what Clem had told him about the law here in Sherman City, about his firm belief that the sheriff himself was working hand in glove with the outlaws and he refrained from asking any further questions. He didn't exactly want the other to know that he had any interest in this at all; not at the moment, anyway. But it was beginning to look as if Clem might have been right, after all. This time, the outlaws had been foiled in their attempt to take the strongbox, but only at the cost of Clem being injured and if anyone was meaning to stop the stageline from operating, that was almost as good a way as any, kill off or wound the drivers and put the girl out of business that way.

Doc Adams climbed out of the coach, glanced up at the sheriff. 'Howdy, Matt. I'll get Clem taken into the depot and fix him up properly there and then I reckon you'll want to ask him some questions.'

The wounded driver was carried into the depot and a couple of men, directed by the sheriff, took the stage around the corner of the building. Then the lawman turned to Cal and the attorney. 'I'd like a word with you two gentlemen,' he said quietly, but in a tone that brooked no argument. 'Mind steppin' along to the office for a few moments?'

'I've got no objection, Sheriff,' said Condor. He gave the lawman a frank stare. 'So long as it doesn't take up too much time. I have a client in town I'm particularly anxious to meet as soon as possible.' He pulled a large gold watch from his pocket and glanced down at it significantly as if to emphasize his anxiety.

'This shouldn't take long,' affirmed the other. 'Just want to ask you both a few questions.' His keen gaze flicked towards Cal questioningly.

The other shrugged. 'I'll naturally do all that I can to help, Sheriff,' he said, 'but there's little I can tell you that you don't already know. Seems to me these hold-ups have been goin' on for some time now.' He fell into step beside the others and pushed his way through the small crowd which was just beginning to disperse.

It was cool and dim inside the sheriff's office with only the paraffin lamp on the table to give any light. The lawman motioned them to chairs and then lowered himself into the tall-backed chair behind the desk. 'I'll tell you both somethin', gents,' he said, rolling himself a smoke. 'I've got a whole heap of suspicions and ideas roostin' around under my hat about this affair. The laws of this state are all writ down in the book but it ain't everybody who has a mind to keep 'em. There's somethin' afoot here that's more'n jest robbin' the stageline, and I'd sure like to know what it is.'

Cal felt a sudden grim amusement in his mind at the other's words. This was a dangerous country and running a stageline could be about the most dangerous job in it. Certainly, on the face of it, it didn't seem to be the job for a woman, even a determined one who wished to follow in her father's footsteps and keep the line moving in spite of everything. Here, a man could only call on gun-law to protect him and his interests and greed was a larger and more demanding thing than even the patient grubbing for gold in the rocks and rivers.

The sheriff looked directly at the attorney. 'I've got a feeling, Mister Condor, that your visit to Sherman City might have some bearin' on this matter.'

'I sincerely hope that you aren't inferring that I have anything to do with these outlaws who attacked the stage,' said the other in a tight, indignant voice.

'Why no — not at all. No offence meant, sir.' The sheriff hesitated for a moment and then settled himself further in his chair. 'I merely meant that according to my information, you came here to see young Scott Kearney. Ain't that so?'

The attorney relaxed visibly in his chair, shoulders slumping a trifle. He nodded slowly. 'I was asked to come here by Mister Kearney, that's quite true,' he admitted, apparently mollified. 'But as you may realize, I cannot discuss any business that I have with him. This is strictly confidential. However, if you were to ask him, I'm quite sure that — '

'I don't think there'll be any real need for that, Mister Condor,' murmured the sheriff. 'Guess almost everyone was lucky this time. They didn't get the strongbox and they lost a couple of men in the attack. Mebbe they'll lay off for a while after this.'

'Depends on what they're really after, I reckon,' said Cal tightly. 'If it's just gold, then they may decide to hightail it out of the territory and look someplace else for easier pickings. On the other hand, that might not be what's in their minds at all.'

'You got any idea what they might be aimin' for?' asked the sheriff.

'Nope. Unless they've been hired by somebody in town to make certain that when Miss Holmes sells the stageline, she's forced to do so for a low price.'

The sheriff's lips quirked into a faint, cold smile. 'Now you ain't got any proof of that, mister,' he remarked quietly. 'And I reckon I'd be doin' you a favour if I warned you that here in Sherman City, folk don't take too kindly to any accusations like that as you'll find out for yourself if you go around passing such remarks. I'm only tellin' you that for your own good seein' as you don't seem to be wearin' any shootin'-irons.'

It was Cal's turn to grin tightly. 'Ain't had any use for 'em so far, sheriff. Seems to me there's often a way of settlin' an argument without havin' to resort to gunplay.'

'Sure, sure,' grunted the other, swivelling in his chair to stare at the window that looked out on to the street as if expecting somebody to come barging in through the door at any moment. He had a habit of turning in his chair as he spoke so that he was never looking directly at the man he addressed. 'But for a man who doesn't believe in gunplay, you sure did well for yourself out there when those outlaws attacked the stage. It ain't all that easy to shoot down a man from the buckboard of a stage when it's movin' like that.'

Cal said nothing in reply to that and a few moments later, the attorney said quietly: 'If you've no further questions to ask me, Sheriff, I'd like to go over to the hotel and see my client before settling in for the night. I'll be only too pleased to tell you anything else I know, should you need my testimony.'

'Don't reckon there'll be any need for that, Mister Condor,' said the other, heaving himself heavily to his feet. For the first time, Cal noticed that the lawman was not as well-muscled as he had thought, that he had allowed himself to run to fat, something that could be fatal for a man in his position, if he really did the job he was paid to do. It brought the little germ of suspicion back in his mind and he found himself wondering if there was anything more behind the other's obvious uneasiness than he yet knew. 'If I do want to talk to either of you again, I reckon I can always find you here in town.'

'Of course,' affirmed Condor quickly. He got to his feet and moved towards the door. Cal followed him, close on his heels, went out into the street. He stood for a moment at the door of the office, drawing the cool night air down into his lungs, then he went across the street towards the hotel. He would have to get a bed for himself too.

This was supper hour and he caught the sudden odour of food as he entered the small lobby and crossed towards the desk. Three men moved out of the dining room, each and all of them giving him a quick glance as they passed; but he was not deceived by the brevity of their stares. They had taken in everything about him, the dust-stained clothes and above all, the fact that he wore no gunbelt. All three men were frocked-coated and one, short and florid-faced, with snow-white whiskers, turned his head and murmured something to his companions as they moved out of the door and into the street. Putting them out of his mind, Cal went over to the desk. Signing his name in the register, he took the key to his room and climbed two flights of stairs to the top floor. Closing the door, he locked it and went over to the window, standing in front of it for a few moments, looking down on to the street, now ablaze with beams of yellow light.

As he watched, a man came striding along the board-walk on the opposite side of the street, his body alternatively in light and shadow as he passed in front of the buildings. Then he paused, stepped out of the shadows, paused for a moment as he threw a swift glance up and down the street, then stepped briskly across the street towards the hotel. He was a tall one, young, with sharp edges to his shoulders and a hard-brimmed Stetson set squarely on his head. Cal caught a brief glimpse of his features as he passed into the beam of light from the doorway almost directly below him.

Cal moved back from the window. There was something about this town, about the whole set-up, which he didn't like. He tried to figure out what it was as he took off his shirt and shook the dust out of it. Then he filled the large porcelain basin from the pitcher and washed the yellow-red dust from his face and neck. It had been hot on top of that rolling stage during the two-day journey and his skin had been scorched by the sun, but he felt better after he had washed and shaved. Putting on a fresh shirt from his bag, he drank his fill of the water still remaining in the pitcher, then made his way down to the dining room, found a place in one corner and leaned back in his chair as he waited for his meal. There was a deep-seated weariness in his body and he deliberately allowed his taut muscles to loosen.

He ate ravenously when the meal came, savouring the well-cooked food, comparing it with that which had been dished up to them at the way station. Pushing his plate away from him, he sipped the hot black coffee, dug in his pocket for the makings of a smoke and in doing so glanced across the room to the far corner. Condor, the attorney, was seated at the table there, his back to him, talking in low tones to the man

Cal had seen enter the hotel when he had been standing at the window of his room. So that was the client Condor had been so anxious to meet. Handsome, but in an arrogant, cruel way. Cal dragged in the sweet cigarette smoke, let it out slowly. For a moment, the other's glance switched from Condor and locked with Cal's, giving him a sharp study. The look quickened Cal's interest and he watched the man's face for a long moment, watching for any sign of change. Then the other looked deliberately away.

Cal smiled grimly to himself as he settled back in his chair. For a moment, there was a sense of restlessness in him and he found his mind flashing back to that heat-filled afternoon when those men had ridden down from the hills of the Snake Pass to attack the stage. Maybe there was more going on here than the townsfolk wanted to talk about, but there was no need for him to get caught up in it, whatever it was. He had come here for the purpose of settling down, maybe buying himself a small spread somewhere close to the town, raising a few head of cattle. The land seemed good here and —

His thoughts broke off. A woman had come into the dining room at that moment and all of his attention had suddenly closed around her as she hesitated in the doorway, looking about her, scanning the faces of the other diners. He guessed she was in her middle twenties, with midnight-black hair which held blue lights as she came forward. Her lips were pressed softly together, almost wilful, her jaw determined. Out of the corner of his eye, he noticed that the man with Condor had half-risen to his feet as he caught sight of her but as her glance fell on him she shook her head ever so slightly, made a faint gesture with her right hand and he sank back into his chair again, a look of vague annoyance on his coldly handsome face. Looking back, Cal saw that her gaze had moved to him, direct and challenging, but with a mute question in it. Her eyes were dark and she continued to watch him as she walked over the room towards him.

'Mister Mannix?' she said swiftly as she paused in front of his table.

For a moment, surprise held him, then he got to his feet a trifle awkwardly. 'Why yes, that's my name, Ma'am.'

Her lips changed, forming a faint smile as she seated herself in the chair opposite him.

He said: 'I'm not sure how you know my name or — '

'Clem told me I might find you here,' she answered. 'I'm Norma Holmes. I own the stageline. I came to thank you for what you did today in fighting off those outlaws who tried to take the strongbox.'

'I reckon anyone would have done the same thing if they'd been in my position and those men attacked the stage he was on. Remember, I was hell-bent on saving my own skin too. I've heard that men like that can do mean and vicious things when they're at the back of a gun.'

She gave him a cool studying glance and for a moment some answer to what he had said was balanced in her mind. Then she shrugged her shoulders slightly and nodded almost imperceptibly. 'You'll have to be careful now, so long as you stay in town. Word travels fast. You see how easy it was for me to find you. You're being watched now; you'll always be watched until they decide what to do with you.'

'They?' He lifted his brows a fraction.

'The men who're trying to destroy everything my father built, everything that I own.'

'You mean that bunch who attacked the coach today.' He gave a brief nod. 'I've heard somethin' about them from Clem. He's quite a talker when he gets goin'.'

'Perhaps he talks a little too much,' said the girl. Her eyes were suddenly troubled. 'They always seem to know every time there's any gold being shipped on the stage.'

'The sheriff mentioned that earlier. Claimed he once took some men with him in the coach and spread the word around that they were haulin' a pretty valuable cargo on that trip. But the outlaws didn't fall for it.'

Norma Holmes nodded. For a moment she stared down at the table in front of her, fingers twisting the cloth. Then she looked up quickly. 'Now that Clem has been shot I don't know how I'll be able to carry on the stageline. Part of the contract for it is that there must be one journey each day and all of my other drivers have either been shot or they've ridden on over the hill.'

Cal tightened his lips. It made sense, he thought inwardly. Men would only take so much of this and then they'd pull out and nothing would induce them to stay. A dead man could never spend any gold that was coming to him. Only anyone as stubborn and as loyal as old Clem would stick by the girl in this time of crisis. He grew aware that the flashily-dressed man with Condor had been watching him closely with a speculative look in his eyes for several moments. Now the other suddenly scraped back his chair, muttered something in a low undertone to the attorney, then came over to Cal's table.

The tall man stopped still, facing the girl. His face hardened a little as he stood there. He said harshly: 'Norma, I'd like to speak to you for a moment. It's important. Attorney Condor is in town and he — '

'Not just now, Scott,' said the girl sharply. Her tone was commanding and imperious. 'I'll talk with you and the attorney tomorrow if you don't mind.'

'And if I do mind?' The other's face showed a deep flush of barely concealed anger under the tan. 'Attorney Condor has come a long way and at short notice to attend to this matter and you owe it to him to show a little civility.' He was very watchful and to Cal, he seemed to be on edge as if he expected some kind of trouble to break out at any moment.

His black coat was thrown back a little, revealing the twin Colts he wore.

Norma Holmes said in her calm, self-assured way: 'I said I'll talk with him later, Scott. At the moment I'm far more concerned about hearing what happened to Clem and the stage today.'

'Don't you think it's a little late to bother your head about that? Clem was a fool to try to bring the stage through.' The other spoke through tight lips. His gaze rested on Cal a long moment as he spoke. 'I warned him against trying to push his luck too far, told him it was sure to give out sooner or later, but he wouldn't listen to reason. Too darned stubborn. Now he's gone and got himself shot because of it.'

'Seems to me some folk in this town might learn a lesson from men such as Clem,' said Cal softly. 'He's the only one who volunteered to keep the stage runnin' in spite of these outlaws.'

Scott Kearney smiled a tight, wintry smile, one that did not reach his eyes and held no mirth in it. 'My advice to you, friend, is to keep out of this. You'd do well to be careful of the kind of men who roam around these hills. This is none of your business and we don't like strangers horning in and putting their noses where they're not wanted.' His glance strayed a little and the smile grew tighter and more unfriendly and there was a faint sneer in his tone as he went on: 'For a man who ain't carryin' any guns, you seem to talk plenty loud, mister.'

'Don't let that fact give you any ideas, Scott,' murmured the girl from the other side of the table. 'He's the man who shot down those outlaws and I reckon he knows how to handle a gun if it's ever necessary.'

There was a new look at the back of the other's eyes at that and they were narrowed just a shade as he muttered: 'I still say it isn't wise to go poking his nose into any of our business.' He turned abruptly on his heel and walked back to his own table, rejoining the little attorney who had been watching the proceedings closely.

Norma Holmes placed her hands on the table and regarded him seriously. 'Well, I think you've made an enemy there, Mister Mannix,' she said quietly. 'He won't forgive you for that, you know.'

'Doubt if I'll lose much sleep over that,' grunted Cal. He finished the coffee in the cup, twisted his face into a faint grimace as the almost cold liquid ran down his throat.

'Maybe not.' Her glance was warmly appraising. 'But he's quite a powerful man in Sherman City and he has a lot of friends among the ranchers.'

Cal was silent for a moment, then he said slowly: 'I guess it's really none of my business, like he says, but just what is he to you, ma'am? I couldn't help noticin' the look he gave you as soon as you stepped into the room and from what he said, I gather there is some kind of a business deal between you.'

The girl bit her lower lip, then nodded. 'Scott has asked me to marry him. He says that with his money and influence, he can make the stageline pay and prevent these frequent hold-ups. He has men who ride with him and they would drive the stages through. Men with guns.'

'And you've agreed to marry him?'

'I've told him that I'll think over his proposal, but I haven't given him a final answer yet.'

Cal rubbed his chin musingly. 'I wonder why he brought Condor here, all the way from Virginia City. I heard him talking to the agent in Red Rock just after we got off the train.'

'Scott wants me to sign the stageline over to him right away. With no one left to drive the coach, I'll be forced to do that. If I don't, then I automatically lose the contract and he'll take it anyway.'

Cal was careful in his reply as he let his gaze drift over to the two men at the far table, now deep in earnest conversation. 'May I ask if he's offered you a fair price for the line?'

The girl pursed her lips for a

moment, then lowered her gize. 'I suppose the price is a fair one when one considers that tomorrow I might get nothing at all, if I lose the contract.'

'So that's the way of things.' Cal's eyes were suddenly hard. 'Doesn't it strike you as strange that Condor was brought in from Virgina City and at the same time, Clem, the only one of your drivers to stick by you, was shot by these outlaws?'

He saw the look at the back of the girl's eyes at this remark, knew that she was thinking along the same lines as himself. 'But you can't mean that Scott is working with these outlaws?'

'It's possible. It won't be the first time a man has thrown in his lot with such *hombres* just to gain his own ends.' He grinned. 'But I reckon we'd be hard put to prove it.'

'I hope you're wrong,' said the girl. She sat silent for a moment, then got to her feet, stood looking down at him for a few seconds, then turned and left the dining room. Cal let his eyes follow her graceful figure until she had vanished through the doorway and into the lobby outside. Then he rolled himself another smoke, aware that Scott Kearney was still eyeing him from across the room, knew that there was a deep hatred in the other's gaze. As Norma Holmes had said, he had already made himself an implacable enemy and he had been in Sherman City only a few hours.

3

Man Behind a Gun

Scott Kearney stepped out on to the upper veranda of the tall hotel and stared down into the street. It was almost dawn and already there was a bar of silver-grey spread across the eastern horizon. Within a few minutes it would turn into a fiery red and then the sun would rise just beyond the range of hills to the north-east. He wondered why his encounter with that man at the table in the dining room, the man they called Cal Mannix, had disturbed him so. It was not only a feeling of anger that rose in his mind, but one of apprehension too; as if he knew, deep inside him, that this man, more than anyone else he had met, could spell trouble for him. The other was not a lawman, he felt certain of that; yet only a man who was supremely confident of himself would walk around a town such as this, or even ride on that stage, without wearing guns. Now, if he had read the signs correctly, Norma had told all of her troubles to this man, besides getting every scrap of information she could from him concerning the attack on the stage. Whether Mannix would try to help her was a debatable point. If it was true that he had come here simply to settle down in this part of the territory, then there was no reason for him to make this any of his business. On the other hand, Norma Holmes could be very persuasive when she wanted to be and there were few men who could resist her charms. Undeniably she was an exceptionally beautiful woman, and she knew it, and she would not be averse to using that beauty to making men do as she wanted them to. She might have been able to talk Mannix into helping her keep the stageline open, although at the moment he did not see how she could do it, except for persuading him to ride the stage for her until she succeeded in getting a regular driver. By now, most of the men who might have agreed to work for her had been scared off by the attacks, but unless he made certain that Mannix didn't cause trouble, he might lose out on this deal even now at the eleventh hour. He had gone to too much trouble and expense to set up this deal to see it slip from his grasp now. For several minutes, he paced up and down the veranda, uneasy and troubled. Until now, he had played his hand well but with caution. He had a thriving lawyer's practice here in Sherman City and there had not been a breath of scandal directed at him. No one suspected that he was in league with the bandits who infested the hills and preyed on the stageline and if he had to marry Norma Holmes to get his hands on that stageline then he was quite prepared to do that, but before that happened, he wanted everything signed over to him, legally and conclusively, and that was why he had sent for Condor. He had known the other during the old days and knew that the man would be trustworthy — for a price. Besides, he himself knew a little too much about Condor for the other ever to dare to defy him.

In the room behind him, Condor was seated in his chair, his face bearing a faintly troubled look also. As Kearney came back into the room, he pushed himself to his feet. 'Are you sure that you can handle the girl, Scott?' he asked quickly. 'I tell you that this man, Mannix, can make trouble for us if he throws in his lot with her. He's a devil with a gun as those outlaws discovered to their cost.'

'Maybe he was plain lucky,' snarled the other, his handsome features contorted by hatred. 'But I want him out of the way before he starts any big trouble for us.'

'That could be a mistake.' Condor's voice was calm.

'Then maybe you have a plan for making sure he doesn't get in our way?' Kearney asked challengingly. His brows were lowered as he stared across the room at the other. When he thought back to Cal Mannix, he felt an angry sense of bafflement, something he couldn't quite put a name to and the memory of that meeting with the other the previous night and how Norma had treated him almost with contempt in front of that stranger rubbed at him like saddle gall. There had to be a way of ridding himself of Mannix without causing too much talk.

'I was watching him during that trip from Red Rock,' murmured Condor, getting to his feet and walking across the room, where he poured himself a drink from the whiskey bottle. He sipped it slowly, savouring it. 'He's a strange man, not easily understood. One who abhors the use of violence, but when the necessity arises, he can use a gun as well as any man I've ever seen.' He picked up the small cigar cutter, snipped the end from a cigar and thrust it between his lips, lighting it with an almost elaborate care, drawing the smoke down deep into his lungs.

'Just what does all that talk mean'?' snapped Kearney. He felt his nerves were rubbed raw by this sudden and unexpected turn of events. Prior to the previous day, everything seemed to be on the point of panning out nicely for him. Now this stranger had to arrive in Sherman City and alter things for him.

'If Miss Holmes does manage to persuade him to work for her until she gets some replacements for the drivers' jobs, we could see to it that he meets with an accident somewhere out of town. I don't like to see violence done myself. As you know, I'm a man of peace, but if it comes to destroying everything that we've worked for all these months, then what's the life of one man compared with all that?'

For a few seconds, Kearney stared at the other in mild surprise. The man's outwardly mild and timid appearance was merely a front which housed a scheming and deliberate mind which would apparently baulk at nothing, even murder.

'Now you're talking like a man after my own heart,' said Kearney harshly, clapping the other on the shoulder. He laughed uncomfortably for a moment, then went on briskly. 'I've made an appointment to see Norma Holmes at nine o'clock sharp. We'll get the answers to some questions then and if our talk with her fails, then we'll do as you suggest.'

* * *

An hour later, Scott Kearney sat in the corner of the living room in the Holmes house and considered Norma Holmes. She seemed to have gained a little more confidence than when he had last spoken to her on this subject a couple of days before and he could guess at the reason for this change in her. Her way of sitting, the level-eyed gaze and the look of composure, reminded him of her father and the devil knew that he had been a stubborn old cuss at the best of times.

He spoke softly even as his critical eyes watched her. 'Runnin' a stageline is a tough business, Norma. You know that and you know that I've offered you a fair price for it, considering the difficulties you find yourself in right now. Today's Sunday, so there's no call to send out the stage, but come tomorrow, it's another matter. What do you reckon on doin' then? Drivin' it yourself?'

'Somehow, I don't think there'll be any need for that,' retorted the girl hotly. 'And I don't intend to sell for the ridiculously low price that you've offered me.'

There was a sharp reply balanced on Scott's tongue, but Condor spoke up quickly. 'I think we have to look at this in a business-like way, Miss Holmes. You can't deny the fact that without any drivers, you don't have a chance of sending out the stage tomorrow — or any other day for that matter. According to the contract which your father signed when he started this line, you have to run the stage in one direction each day. We know that you have no drivers. Most of them have upped and left rather than run the risk of being killed by these outlaws. The law here seems unable to prevent these attacks and to be quite honest, I can't see you hirin' anybody in time to fulfil the requirements of the contract. You have no choice. Either you accept Mister Kearney's generous offer to buy you out and put the stageline back into business, or you're forced to give it up completely.'

Kearney smiled with some indulgence. 'That's puttin' it plain, Norma. Won't you try to see sense?'

She looked at him intently. 'Scott,' she said, 'I can read your mind. I've known you for a good many years. You're sorrowing with me today, making it seem that you're doing all of this just to help me in a tough spot. But I can see why you want the stageline. You're hoping to be a big man in this part of the territory. You've already put yourself into a high position with the bank, I guess, and it doesn't take much to realize that you're probably behind one or two of the gambling saloons in town. But like most people here I've shut my eyes to that because it hasn't interfered with me. But in spite of what is happening now, I mean to do what my father tried to do when he was alive.'

'What's that?'

'Build up this stageline, even in opposition to the railroad. Sooner of later, the railroad will squeeze out all the overland routes we have now, but that time isn't yet and it won't come for ten, maybe twenty, years. Long enough for me to build up the line into what my father dreamed it would be.'

Kearney stared at her, surprised a little by the vehemence and the grim determination in her voice. It irritated him to know that she understood and knew more about his activities in town than he had thought. He said pointedly: 'The truth is, Norma, that after tomorrow, you won't have a stageline. You can keep it with my help, not otherwise. Don't let your fancies and dreams get the better of you.'

She studied him over a short thoughtful interval, her face cold and tight. 'You seem to be very blunt when you know that you don't have to be charming to me,' she said. 'But you don't know me quite as well as you believe and you'll never be certain what I mean to do next, nor where exactly I stand.'

Kearney leaned forward in his chair. He was trying to judge her, to figure her out for himself and he was having a poor time of it. She had changed in a great many ways over the past two days and was now throwing all of his reasoning out of line.

'Do I take it that you're turning down my offer, Norma?'

'Yes. I've already hired a driver. He'll

take out the stage tomorrow.'

Kearney narrowed his eyes to mere slits. 'Not that man you were talking with in the hotel last night? The man who came in on the stage with Condor here.'

'That's right. I hired him first thing this morning.'

'That wasn't a very wise thing to do,' he said, very softly and slowly. 'A man who doesn't wear guns, who doesn't like violence. He'll probably run at the first sign of trouble next time. Sure, he seemed brave enough yesterday when he had to shoot to save his own skin. But will he risk his life every day just to keep you in business?'

'I think he will,' said the girl evenly. 'I don't believe that he'll run like the others.'

Heavily, a scowl on his features, Kearney pushed back his chair and got to his feet. He said sharply, 'Only time will tell, Norma and I hope for your sake that you're right about him. But you're makin' a very big mistake not taking my offer. The next time, I'll just wait and then step in and take it over for nothing.' He whirled on his heel and walked angrily to the door. 'Let's get out of here, Condor,' he said through tightly-clenched teeth. 'I can see that we're wasting our time right now.'

'Perhaps,' murmured Condor softly, as he moved across the room, 'this man might be persuaded to change his mind. After all, I'm sure that not all of the disadvantages — or advantages — have been pointed out to him.'

Kearney grinned, lips thinned. 'You may have something there,' he nodded, his eyes fixed on the girl. 'I suggest that we pay a call on Mister Mannix and point out some of the advantages to him of not riding the stage tomorrow.'

* * *

The shadows were still long and the sun had only just lifted clear of the horizon when Cal came to the summit of the trail, reined his mount and sat tall in the saddle for a long moment, perusing the terrain that lay ahead of him. He guessed that he had another five miles to cover before he reached Snake Pass and at any point along that trail, he might be under observation from the rocks that bordered it on both sides. He had ridden out of Sherman City shortly after dawn, just after he had finally accepted the job of driver on the stage which left town the next morning on its way through to Red Rock. Even now, he was still surprised at himself for accepting the job. It wasn't just that he wanted to help the girl out of this tight spot, nor that he wished simply to see that justice was done in this case. There was something more to it than that, but at the moment he was unable to put his finger on it. He forced himself up a little higher in the saddle, narrowing his eyes against the savage red glare of the rising sun. There was no sign of life, of movement, among the rocks that lay tumbled along the flanks of the trail where it wound and twisted its way up into the rocks. There was therefore nothing he could do but continue to ride until he came to Snake Pass and scout around, see if he could find any evidence of where those outlaws might have their hideout.

He also wanted to see for himself whether they had come back for the bodies of the men he had killed. If they had, it seemed as good an indication as any that they had not lit out for other parts. Gigging his mount, he set it at a quick gallop along the trail. He remembered some of the landmarks from that last ride with the stage and in the growing brilliance of dawn, he was able to make out the rising trail where it cut up into the higher reaches of the mountain, with Snake Pass just visible at the far end. Beyond that point, he knew, the trail dipped downward towards the desert and it was inconceivable that the outlaws would try to cross that vast stretch of alkali and red dust. Their hiding place would be somewhere up there among the rocks where they could watch the trail for several miles in either direction and plan their ambushes accordingly.

As he rode, his nerves became taut. There was a deep and clinging silence over everything which only served to increase his tension. He rode through the brush and foothills without seeing anything suspicious, then began the long climb to the pass now clearly visible in the distance. Already, there was a heat in the air and the outlines of the rocks and peaks began to shimmer in the distance. Half an hour later, he rode into the stretch of trail where the bodies of the men he had shot down had lain. He reined in at the side of the trail, eyes searching for them. But they were no longer there and his suspicions began to harden into a certainty in his mind. In spite of this setback, the outlaws clearly intended to carry on with their raids against the stages if anyone continued to bring them through. At least he knew where he stood now. He turned over the various possibilities in his mind, riding slowly forward along the narrow trail which ran beside a rising slope of rock. Ten minutes later, he reached a narrow belt of timber and suddenly came upon a trail that led off the main stage route, up into the hills. Pausing, he scanned it carefully. It was a trail he had not noticed during that running fight with the outlaws; but that was to be expected, he decided abruptly. It ran back in the direction of Snake Pass and it would easily have been missed by a man on the stage, even if there had been no other distractions.

Setting his mount at the slope, he rode slowly along the winding trail, eyes alert, every nerve and fibre in his body taut with expectation. There was no doubt in his mind that this was one of a multitude of trails that criss-crossed these hills, used by the men who inhabited this area. Wind flowed downhill with a faint cooling pressure against him and he was glad of it as the heat head continued to intensify. There was a small cluster of trees at the rim of a low ridge directly ahead of him and acting on impulse, he reined his mount and slid out of the saddle, moving forward on foot. He knew nothing of these hills or the short trails there might be here and he was forced to move with caution for fear of being jumped when he least expected it. With an effort, he fought his way over some of the roughest footing he had ever known, moved over the crest of the ridge, across a fresh slide of loose packed dirt, then down into a narrow gully that led like a grey scar down the side of the ledge.

This was the way of it for half an hour. Then, at the bottom of the ravine where it opened out again into a stretch of scree-covered ground, he paused abruptly. There was the sharp, unmistakable smell of smoke hanging in the air and moments later, he caught the sound of wood crackling in the near distance. Cautiously, he edged forward, topped a low rise then found himself looking down on the small campfire that had been built in the middle of a small clearing, surrounded by rocks. He stood quite still, feeling his danger. There was no one near the fire but he knew instinctively that whoever had made it, was somewhere close by, that they had in all probability watched him come up and were keeping a watch on him at that very moment, possibly laying a gun on him.

There was no point in being too cautious now. He stood up and went forward, until he stood by the fire. A little spot between his shoulder blades began to ache and a moment later, he heard the solid scrape behind him, the sound of boots on the rock, then a man came into view beside him, moving forward; a man who carried a rifle in his right hand, but it was no longer pointed at him and he felt a little easier in his mind.

'Ain't you a little off the beaten track,

mister?' growled the other after a short pause, moving around to the other side of the fire where he could watch Cal more closely. Shaggy, black brows were drawn down over the other's eyes and his hair was unkempt, matted a little under the greasy, stained hat that hung floppily over his ears.

'Could be,' acknowledged Cal softly. 'You been here long?'

'Long enough.' The other seated himself on an outcrop of rock and motioned Cal to do likewise. 'Out here, there's nobody to worry me. I do just as I please without havin' to answer to anybody.'

Just another drifter, thought Cal inwardly, with a great sense of relief, another of the lost men who sought the sanctuary of these hills and mountains, all running from someplace or other, keeping one jump ahead of the law. Hunted like dogs, and never knowing any real place of refuge, always moving on over the mountains as they tried to find some trail that would lead them to safety. A break one way had thrown this man on the wrong side of the law at some time or another, and possibly a succession of bad breaks had kept him drifting deeper and deeper like a steer in quicksand, until he was no longer able to pull himself clear. He thought about it for a moment and was vaguely troubled; then he put the thought out of his mind. This was the path the other had chosen or circumstances had thrust upon him and it was no business of his to try to force him out on to another trail.

'Don't suppose you've seen anythin' of a bunch of outlaws who've been infestin' these parts, have you?'

'Nope.' The other shook his head slowly, but emphatically, bent forward and lifted the tin can from above the fire and poured out coffee into a mug which he gave to Cal. 'I've more sense than to interfere with the likes of them. I've found that if I leave them alone, they usually do the same for me.'

Cal drew in a deep gust of air, sipped

the scalding hot coffee. It brought a little of the life back into his body and he felt better after he had washed some of the dust out of his mouth and throat.

'You lookin' for 'em for some particular reason, mister?' asked the other shrewdly.

'They tried to hold up the stage bound for Sherman City a couple of days ago. I was on it at the time and I thought I'd backtrack and see if I could pick up anythin'. I always like to know who comes a-gunnin' for me.'

'Reckon you'd do better to leave well alone, not to try and stir things up any more.'

'Like now?' said Cal, watching the look in the other's eyes. The man was obviously on tenterhooks, unsure of himself. Cal could see it in the way he kept switching his glance from side to side, scanning the hills and rocks that lay in tumbled heaps all about them. There was no doubt that this man knew where the outlaws were, but he would never talk.

The man nodded, then switched the subject. 'How'd you like bacon and beans for breakfast? Got plenty of grub here and I can always shoot a deer or get some fish for myself in the river back yonder a piece.'

'Thanks all the same, but I figure I'd better make tracks back to town.' Cal rose to his feet, stood for a moment drawing air down into his lungs. The worst of the day was yet to come and there was a lot of riding ahead of him. The other's offer was tempting, but there were several answers to a lot of burning questions that he wanted and he would only have a few hours in which to find some of them. Tomorrow morning, at first light, he was due to take the stage out of Sherman City and along this trail all the way into Red Rock, and then back again. In that four-day period, he hoped that the girl would have been able to settle her quarrel with Kearney and hire more drivers. Whatever happened, he only intended this to be a temporary thing.

He had only one desire in his mind, to settle down in Sherman City, not to act as driver for the stageline.

'Watch your step in these hills, mister,' said the other, without getting to his feet. 'Like you say, there are men here who have the ways of wolves and if they once suspect you're after 'em, you won't leave here alive. I notice you're not carryin' any guns. Could be a mistake. They ain't got any ethics here.'

'Thanks for the warning — and the coffee,' nodded Cal. He moved back along the track, came up to where he had left his mount and swung up easily into the saddle. He rode over the rock floor of the wide bowl of ground, then back on to the main trail, cutting up through Snake Pass to the point where he could pause and look out over the stretching flatness of the desert. Nothing moved in the heat-shimmering wildness; not that he had expected to see anyone out there. A man would be visible for miles in that terrible emptiness. At the first, convenient spot, he wheeled his horse up into the rocks, climbing higher so that he might look out over the rocks and down on to the trail where it snaked back through the Pass towards Sherman City. He was now almost five hundred feet above the trail and halted his mount there, leaning forward with his elbows on the saddle horn, letting his mount blow. Sweat beaded his forehead and trickled down the folds of his skin, mingling with the dust that had laid a mask on his face. From this point, as he rode slowly back to Sherman City, he wished to keep close to the rim of the hills so that he might see all that went on down below him.

Near mid-afternoon, he caught a sudden glimpse of movement far below and drew his mount a little further from the rim so that he might not be silhouetted on the skyline. The canyon below made a slow curve to the northwest, the far wall remaining almost sheer for virtually all of its length. But closer at hand, immediately below him, the rocks fell away in a steadier drop and it was down there, on a wide, smooth ledge, that he caught a fragmentary glimpse of the solitary rider, pushing his mount at a cruel pace. It was impossible to recognize the man from that distance, but there was something oddly familiar about him that struck Cal at once and he felt certain that he had met up with the other someplace recently. He sat tall in the saddle, trying to figure out who the other might be, then gave it up and concentrated all of his attention of watching the man. The dust kicked up by the pounding hoofs of the rider's horse laid a line of grey all the way behind him, settling slowly in the still air, making it a relatively simple thing to follow him all the way along the trail and then up into the rocks that bordered it for a goodly length. Finally, the other rode into the tumbled boulders almost directly below the ledge on which Cal had halted his own mount and vanished from sight in a narrow, shadowed pass. Cal waited for several moments for the other to come back into sight again at the far end, but he never did and at last, he gigged his mount forward, a puzzled frown on his features. It could be that this was where the outlaws had their hideaway. Possibly there was a cavern of sorts down there, hidden from view by the rocky overhang of the pass. It would be virtually impossible to make it out from where he was but he swung his gaze slowly from one side to the other, taking in all of the landmarks, knowing that he would be able to find that place again if the necessity ever arose.

By now, the sun was past its zenith and beginning its slow westward drop down the cloudless mirror of the heavens. He turned his mount back to the north-west, headed it back in the direction of town. He doubted if he could discover anything more out here and he still had several things to think out before he reached town. That man he had spotted. Evidently the other had known that trail intimately which indicated that there was some link between him and the outlaws. If only he could remember where he had seen the other before. Certainly it had not been Scott Kearney, nor the little attorney, both of whom seemed to be in this rotten deal up to their necks. But who else was there, who might be in cahoots with the outlaws?

It came to him who that man had been half an hour later as he came down from the hills and hit the main trail some ten miles out from Sherman City. It had been the sheriff from Sherman City and he had not been riding into the outlaw's stronghold to bring them in for trial. He had ridden that trail like a man who had known it for years and that fact alone damned him in Cal's eyes.

★　★　★

Cal left his mount at the livery stable and made his way to the Holmes' place in one of the side roads that led off the main street of town. There was a well in the back yard behind the house and a wooden bucket hanging from the rope. He paused there for a moment and ladled the cool clear water from it, drinking thirstily. The water gurgled down his throat and washed the dust from his mouth, slaking his thirst. The back door of the house opened a moment later and he glanced up to see the girl come out on to the porch, stand there in the open doorway looking across at him before stepping down and walking over.

'Did Scott or that attorney friend of his speak to you today, Cal?' she asked pointedly.

He shook his head, a little surprised. 'Been out of town since early mornin' in the hills at Snake Pass,' he explained. 'Why — were they lookin' for me?'

'They came to see me just after we'd spoken this morning. They wanted to buy the stageline. Scott made the same offer as before, but I refused it.'

'I'm glad you did.'

'But thinking back on it, I'm not sure now that I did the right thing after all. Perhaps they were right when they said I'm finished. I can't get any men to work for me and it isn't fair to ask you to go on like this, especially after you told me the plans you had when you came here.'

'They can wait,' he said quietly, but with a hardness in his tone that was unintended. 'I've been learnin' quite a lot of things today; things I only guessed at yesterday.'

'And they've made you change your mind a little?' The girl took him by the arm and they walked side by side into the house.

'You've ridden a long way.' Norma said as he sank down in to one of the chairs. 'I'll get you a bite to eat.' She showed him an expression that meant nothing and then went through into the kitchen where he heard her moving pots and pans around. Soon there was the appetising aroma of bacon frying in the pan and the muscles of his mouth and jaw jumped a little at the odour. Not until she had placed the meal before him and was seated in the chair opposite him did he speak.

'I reckon I've got the outlaws' hideout tagged, up there in the hills above Snake Pass.'

'What does that mean? That you want to get men together and ride out there with the sheriff for a showdown with them?'

He shook his head, chewed reflectively on a mouthful of food for a long moment before answering. 'That would solve nothin', I'm afraid. I wasn't certain before how these owlhoots were gettin' their information. Now I'm reasonably sure. I saw a man spurring his horse along one of the short trails in the hills. He went straight to their hideout without pausing once like he was an old hand at that game.'

'Did you see who it was?' There was a faint note of emotion in the girl's voice which he couldn't quite place. It wasn't exactly fear, nor apprehension; but a curious tightness that told him nothing.

'I didn't recognize him at first; but I knew there was something familiar about him. It was the sheriff.'

The girl sat bolt upright in her chair, staring at him. 'Are you sure? But it couldn't have been him. Why he's — '

'He's supposed to be the law in this town,' said Cal grimly. He nodded, pushed away the empty plate, sat back in his chair. 'You'd really be surprised how many supposed lawmen are really in cahoots with these outlaws. In many places their siding with these killers is so blatant that they have to be removed. But our friend here is playing it safe and careful. My guess is that he went high-tailin' it out there to warn 'em that the stage would be rollin' at dawn tomorrow and they'll be waitin' for it.'

The girl's face was serious and troubled. 'I've got to keep this stageline

111

moving, Cal. 1 don't want to be driven out.'

'We can try. At least we're forewarned too.' He forced a quick, grim smile.

'What do you intend to do?'

He inclined his head gravely. 'I'm not sure at the moment. Unless I miss my guess, I'll have a visit from Kearney and Condor before nightfall.'

'I'm sure you will.' Her eyes appraised him solemnly in the dim light. 'They aren't sure of you at the moment. You're something of a mystery to them and they don't know how far you'll go if it comes to a showdown. They'll want to make certain about that before they finalize any plans they've made.'

Cal raised his brows a little. 'Then you're convinced that Scott Kearney is working in cahoots with these outlaws who're strivin' to ruin you?'

'I don't know. Everything is so mixed up at the moment that I don't know what to think. If all of this is true, I don't know how I ever thought I could love a man like Scott.'

'He's good-lookin',' suggested Cal meaningly. He noticed the faint flush that rose to her face and she turned her head away slightly as if to prevent him noticing her embarrassment. 'Trouble is that he may be too ambitious and ruthless when it comes to gettin' what he wants. I've known men like that. They will let nothin' stand in their way. Sometimes they're more dangerous than the polecats who roam the hills and make their pickin' by robbing the stages and rustlin' cattle.'

He sat for a moment, then pushed back his chair and rose lithely to his feet. 'Thanks for the meal, Norma,' he said easily. 'Reckon I'd better go and have a word with Kearney. I'll drop around at dawn tomorrow.'

'Be careful.' She spoke in a faint whisper. 'You're the only one who can help me now.'

He moved over to the door. 'I'll take a look in on Clem on the way,' he promised. 'When he's back on his feet again, I've no doubt he'll want to ride that trail again.'

Out in the street, he made his way slowly to the hotel, keeping his eyes open as he walked, booted heels making dull echoes on the wooden boardwalk. The sun was dying in a blaze of scarlet behind the mountains in the west. It would be dark within the hour. Here, there was very little twilight as he had found out for himself riding in the desert and the hills. Several of the men spoke to him as he strolled the length of the street. Word of what he had offered to do would have spread quickly in a town such as this and most of the townsfolk here were decent people who wanted only to be left in peace. It was a small handful of men who tried to run the town in their own crooked way who were causing all of the trouble. The ways of violence never seemed to change out here on the frontier, always the same. Men set themselves up against others; cattle was rustled and

114

run off the plains into the hills; the stages were robbed, banks robbed, their safes cleared of gold and currency, even the trains on the railroad were being held up by the bandit gangs who flourished in this territory. The wild, lawless ones who stooped to violence and death to gain their own ends. And there were always men such as Scott Kearney, decent to begin with, but fired by a passion and ambition that forced them into evil ways. Men who remained mainly in the background of things, running the law from the shadows. It was a relatively simple matter to hunt down and destroy most of the outlaw gangs. In the end they usually got their just deserts, but men like this were different. Faceless men, who wielded the real power, who built towns and cities and grew strong, wealthy and powerful by grinding others into the dirt, buying them out for a miserly sum in certain instances, running them out at other times, sometimes resorting to murder when all else failed.

He was on the point of stepping across the street towards the hotel when he paused and drew back swiftly into the shadows. The sheriff came riding swiftly along the street, throwing up a cloud of dust behind him. He reined in front of the lawyer's office a few blocks away from the hotel, tossed the reins over the hitching rail and ran inside, slamming the glass-fronted door behind him.

Still in the shadows, Cal made himself a smoke and leaned his shoulder against the wooden wall of the building, watching the office across the street. Smoking made his presence there inconspicuous and no one gave him a second glance as he waited to see what would happen. The sheriff would have ridden hell for leather from the outlaws' hideout after talking things over with them, the fact that he had ridden straight to Scott Kearney's office to report strengthened the link between the young lawyer and the outlaws. If he had had any doubts about this earlier, they were gone now.

When ten minutes had gone and there was still no sign of the sheriff coming out, he tossed the butt of the cigarette on to the dusty street, pushed himself upright and stepped down. There was little point in waiting any longer and he wanted to have a word with Clem anyway. He found the little driver lying back in the long bed in the rear room of the house along one of the narrow streets. A harness of bandage was looped around his back and shoulder, anchoring a pad of cotton that lay on his back. He had one arm thrown out behind his head and his lips thinned back into a welcoming grin as he saw who it was, peering forward in the faint light from the lantern on the small table beside the bed.

'Howdy, pardner,' he welcomed. 'Figgered yuh's be along sometime. Reckon there must be plenty o' trouble blowin' up in town, eh?'

'Plenty,' nodded Cal, seating himself in the chair by the bed. 'And Miss

Holmes seems to be slap in the middle of it.'

The other sobered instantly. 'That's what I reckoned might happen,' he said seriously. He rubbed the white whiskers, grimaced. 'If only I could get up outa this bed, I'd take that stage out tomorrow.'

'I've agreed to take it out, old-timer. Set your mind easy about that.'

The other stared at him. 'Yuh mean to drive it to Red Rock and back? D'yuh know what yuh'd be headin' into out there?'

'I guess so. I rode out this mornin' and took a look-see. Some activity in the hills near Snake Pass where they jumped us the other day. Saw the sheriff high-tailin' it out there too. He's back in town now. Came ridin' in a coupla minutes ago and went straight to young Kearney's office.'

Clem's eyes narrowed to mere slits at that piece of news, but there was little surprise showing on his grizzled face as he tried to heave himself upright in the

118

bed. He almost made it, was then forced to lie back on the pillow with a groan.

He nodded his head slowly. 'Yuh big enough to hold 'em off if they do come again? They'll be ready the next time. Reckon we were kinda lucky to drive 'em off when we did.'

'There ain't nobody else in town who'll take the stage through and if it don't go out on schedule, Miss Norma loses the contract.'

'An' that's what they're sittin' back and waitin' fer,' grunted the other. He sucked in a deep gust of air, lay back and stared up at the ceiling over his head for a long moment. The breath brought a fresh stab of agony into his shoulder and he bared his teeth for a moment, the outflung hand gripping the bedpost and tightening on it until the muscles in his arm stood out like cords under the gnarled flesh. 'Give me a week and I'll be up on my feet again, ready to ride with yuh, Cal.' He blinked his eyes several times, then went on.

'Yuh know, when yuh rode that stage with me outa Red Rock, I had yuh figgered for some kinda dude, scared to handle a gun. But yuh'll need one now if yuh're to stay alive. They won't let yuh live now yuh've taken sides with Miss Norma.'

'So I've figgered. Kearney wants to have a word with me apparently. He's been lookin' for me all over town today. When he gets through with the sheriff, he'll try to find me and talk me out of this. When that doesn't work, he'll try to scare me off and then those outlaws will be waitin' for me near Snake Pass.'

Clem shook his head, the white beard shining a little in the lantern light. 'Can't help you none right now, I'm afraid. An' there ain't anybody in town who'd ride with yuh as shotgun.'

'I guessed that much,' said Cal grimly. 'Just you get well, Clem and then we can fight this thing together.'

Clem said in a gritty voice: 'Don't let the fact that yuh shot down two or three of 'em throw yuh. There's more polecats in them hills than yuh can count, an' they hang together like flies.' He scowled up at the ceiling as if seeking words, and added: 'Too many funny things have been happenin' around here. Pity we ain't got a decent sheriff, a straight-shooter.'

He lay over on his side, nodded towards the pitcher on the table. 'Just pour me a glass of water, Cal. Reckon I can sleep now. Lots of things have been troublin' me while I've lain here today, tryin' to think things out.'

Cal gave him the glass of water, watched while he sipped it slowly, then put the empty glass back on the table and moved silently out of the room closing the door gently behind him. Outside, it was almost dark. The last vestiges of red were being swamped rapidly in the west as the night came in from the east, over the desert. There was a coolness in the street now, a faint breeze that blew against his face, easing away a little of the tension that had built up inside him. There was a faint light in the lawyer's office, but it was extinguished as he drew almost level with it and a second later, the door opened and Kearney stepped out on to the boardwalk, caught a glimpse of him and said loudly:

'Ah, Mister Mannix. I've been looking all over town for you. Want to have a little chat with you if I may.' He locked the office behind him as he spoke, then stepped down in to the street and fell in step with Cal.

'I don't think we have anythin' in common to talk about,' said Cal quietly.

The other smiled, his teeth white in the shadow of his face. He did not seem to have been touched by the lack of friendliness in Cal's statement.

'On the contrary, I believe we have a lot in common and it may be to your interest.'

'Talk's cheap,' acknowledged the other. He followed Kearney through the doors of the hotel and into the bar. The lawyer led him to a small table in one corner, well away from the others, a place where they could talk without any fear of their conversation being overheard. The barkeep came over quickly as Kearney gave a sharp order, brought back the bottle of whiskey and two glasses which he set down on the table in front of them, then withdrew at a curt order from Kearney as the other settled back in his chair.

Pouring out two glasses of the liquor, Kearney picked up his own glass and murmured softly: 'Let's drink a toast. To progress, Mister Mannix.'

Cal grinned slightly, 'I'll drink to that,' he agreed. He tossed back the raw liquor.

'Now, let's get down to business,' went on the other, leaning forward and resting his elbows on the table. He lowered his voice still further. 'I hear that Norma Holmes has asked you to ride stage for her tomorrow so that she can keep the contract for the stageline.'

'That's right.' With an effort, Cal kept all emotion out of his tone.

'And you agreed to do so?'

'Yes.' He reached out for the bottle and poured another drink for himself, keeping his gaze fixed on the other's face as he did so.

'Don't you think that was a little — ah, foolish? After all, three drivers have been shot dead in the past few months and old Clem was wounded the last time out. Besides, I understand there's a lot more to driving a stage than might seem at first sight. You done this kind of work before?'

'No. But it seems to me there's nobody else in town who's man enough to do the job.'

'Why risk your own neck? This is no affair of yours. Those hills out there are the haunt of all the wild ones in the territory. Every stage that rolls through is fair bait for them and they often don't stop to ask questions. They reckon that dead men tell no tales and — '

'Isn't it true that you want this stageline yourself, Mister Kearney? I understand you've offered to buy it. If that's so, how do you intend to make sure that these owlhoots don't continue to hold it up?'

The other watched him narrowly for a few seconds, seemed to have been taken by surprise by the direct question, then he forced a quick smile, said: 'You evidently don't know much about my standing in this town, Mannix. Not only am I the lawyer here, but I also own one of the biggest spreads in the territory. I've got more than forty men I can call to me at any time. I figure that with them at my back, I could get that stage through every time without too much trouble from these outlaws. Once they realize that they don't stand a chance of holding it up, they'll soon move out to fresh fields.'

Cal drew his brows together. 'That seems a fair enough answer,' he agreed. He sipped his drink slowly this time, watching the other over the rim of the glass. 'But there are still a few things that are puzzlin' me.'

'Such as?'

'They tell me that you and Norma Holmes were goin' to be married pretty soon. Why not help her now, get your men to ride with the stage until she's on her feet once more. Seems to be you're hellbent on driving her out of business and maybe out of town by the way you're actin' now.'

Kearney's face grew suddenly hard and his lips twisted into a faint sneer of anger. 'Until you rode into Sherman City, Mannix, that was going to be the case. It would have been advantageous to us both, but she seems to have got uppity about it quite sudden. Wants to continue on her own.'

'In other words, you want that stageline by any means and if marriage isn't goin' to be the way, then you'll take other steps.'

Kearney splashed more whiskey into his glass, gulped it down quickly, then poured another drink but left it standing in front of him this time, untouched. 'You seem bent on making trouble here, don't you, Mannix,' he

126

gritted through clenched teeth. 'Just where do you fit into all this? I heard you'd come here to Sherman City to settle down, maybe buy yourself a small spread nearby and raise a few head of cattle. Why poke your nose into my business?'

'Could be because I don't like to see injustice bein' done, especially to a lady. Another thing, I don't like crooked lawmen.'

Kearney lifted his head sharply, lips tight. 'Just what d'you mean by that?' he snapped. All pretence at friendliness had vanished now, the thin mask of amiability stripped bare, revealing him as he really was, cold and ruthless.

Cal shrugged. 'I was riding the hills above Snake Pass today, Kearney,' he said slowly, 'just checking on the scene of the attack. I figgered that maybe if those dead outlaws were still lyin' there by the trail, it could mean the others had decided to throw in their hand and had ridden out. But they'd been taken away and buried someplace, so I guess I was wrong on that score.'

'So?'

'Then I got to riding the ridges above the pass and it was then I spotted the sheriff below me on one of the short trails in the hills. He seemed to be in an almighty hurry but his dust followed him and I spotted where he went. He seems to know those trails pretty well.'

'Just what is it you're tryin' to say?' grated Kearney. His hand around the glass had tightened convulsively, knuckles standing out whitely under the skin.

'Ain't nobody up in them hills but outlaws. You said so yourself. Now why should the sheriff want to ride out to see them? Don't reckon he'd be fool enough to ride into their hideout by himself to make an arrest, so I figure that he's on more than noddin' terms with 'em.'

Kearney scraped back his chair, got heavily to his feet, stood looking down at Cal. There was a murderous look on his face as he said raspingly: 'I notice you still ain't carrying any guns,

Mannix. Maybe you figure that might save you. It won't, believe me. And if you ride that stage out of here tomorrow morning, it'll be the last ride you ever take, I promise you that. I've tried to reason with you, but you're like Clem, too goddamned stubborn and foolish. We don't want your kind around Sherman City and I reckon we know how to take care of you.'

Cal grinned slightly, locked his gaze with the other's. 'I wouldn't be too sure of that, Kearney,' he said with a deliberate softness, his voice very low. 'There have been other men who have tried that, but as you see, I'm still around to tell the tale.'

Kearney uttered a harsh laugh. 'You talk big now, Mannix,' he said thinly. 'But we'll see how you talk in a little while.' Turning on his heel, he walked out of the room. Cal sat quite still at the table, then poured another drink and sat back. There was a tightness in his mind now that he knew where he stood with these men. The cards were on the table and he did not doubt that a hard fight lay ahead of him. Whether or not the odds were too great, he did not know. One man stood very little chance against the forces which these ruthless men could bring to bear. Yet he had given his word to the girl and he knew that somehow, whatever happened, he would have to go through with it.

4

Stage Ride

There was no one in the lobby of the hotel when he came down the following morning, but it was still early, not yet sun-up. He looked around, then glanced into the dining room, but it was also empty, with the tables laid ready for breakfast in about an hour. There was no point in waiting and he had plenty to do before dawn. One of the saloons was open on Whiskey Row and he went inside for a quick meal. The food was not cooked as well as that at the hotel, but he was hungry and it was the best he would get at that early hour. At the stage depot, he checked that the coach was ready and that the horses were being attended to, then stepped along the main street until he came to the hardware store which he had noticed the previous day. He had already ascertained that it contained a gunshop. The store was not open when he arrived but by knocking loudly on the door he succeeded in rousing the owner.

'We ain't open for another hour,' muttered the other surlily. He eyed Cal curiously, then his mouth opened slackly. He stood a little on one side without a further word and let him enter, closing the door quickly behind him after taking a furtive glance along the street in both directions to make certain that it was empty.

'Yuh're that *hombre* who's ridin' the stage out to Red Rock today, ain't yuh? I reckoned I recognized yuh.'

'That's right,' Cal nodded. There was a rifle on the stage, the one he had used before, but he bought a couple of packets of shells for it, stuffed them into his pockets, then examined the Colts which the other had in stock. If this town wanted to see him wearing guns then they would, he thought grimly.

The gunsmith watched him as he checked the weapons there. This shop bought and sold guns every day of the week, including Sundays, and the buying of weapons generally occasioned little, or no, interest. But these were not the normal trading hours and it was well known that he was a man who usually wore no guns. He finally chose a pair of matched Colts, bought himself a gunbelt to match and cartridges for the weapons. The man eyed him closely as he buckled on the heavy belt, then cleaned and oiled the guns for him, handing them over the counter when he had finished.

'You know how to use these guns?' asked the man quietly. He came around the edge of the counter. 'They're a pretty tough bunch in the hills, and even in town there are men like 'em.'

'I've already found that out for myself,' Cal assured him, nodding. He moved to the door, opened it and stepped out. It was still dark, with the stars shining brightly overhead, fading just a little towards the east. The houses and stores stood out darkly against the sky, with only a few lights beginning to show in the windows of the saloons, further along the street. A horse snickered faintly from the direction of the livery stable and a moment later, a man came out of the dark shadows and stood with his shoulders against one of the posts. There was the brief flare of a match as he lit a cigarette.

He must have caught a glimpse of Cal for he called softly: 'You're up early, friend. It ain't dawn yet.'

'Got plenty to do before then,' muttered Cal. He went over to the other, stood in the cool darkness and rolled a smoke himself, lit it and drew the sweet smoke down into his lungs, relaxing a little.

'They tell me that some danged fool is goin' to ride the stage outa town this mornin',' grunted the other, evidently not recognizing Cal. 'Can't say I envy him his job. Wouldn't take it on myself for a year's pay.'

'You reckon he'll never make it?' asked Cal, professing some interest.

'Too true he won't.' The man grinned wolfishly. 'There's too many waiting out there to stop him.' He drew on his cigarette, the tip glowing redly in the darkness. 'Heard he's a stranger here. Mebbe he don't know the set-up in these parts. Still — ' he shrugged his shoulders nonchalently. 'I guess he won't live long enough to rake in his first week's pay.'

'Is that what they say?'

The man turned to glance more closely at him. 'Reckon it is,' he affirmed. The dawn was beginning to brighten in the east now, a bar of silver laid low over the skyline. The outlines of the buildings on either side of the street showed more clearly. Sherman City was coming awake. A couple of men stepped into view from one of the buildings and strolled side by side into the hotel. Further along the street, the agent from the stage depot came out and began to adjust the lashings of the coach, intent on his work. Another hour, thought Cal inwardly, and the stage would roll out of town and on into danger. Whether or not there were any passengers who would have the guts to ride with it, he didn't know. It was more than likely that they would go to the railhead and take the train back into Red Rock; a far quicker journey and a more uneventful one. On the other hand, there might be some who would want to come along for the ride and see how this new man made out in the face of danger, knowing that the outlaws would be gunning only for him and that so long as they carried no valuables themselves, they were unlikely to lose much.

Grinding out the butt of his cigarette, he moved away and drifted back into the hotel. The clerk was behind the desk now and he stared in surprise at Cal as the other walked in, watched as he went up the stairs to his room. He stood in front of the window and watched the activity down in the street below. First the sheriff put in an appearance, stepping out of his office and moving slowly towards the saloon. He stood for several minutes on the steps and eyed the hotel, sweeping his glance over the windows that fronted the street, but Cal had already stepped further into the room and he knew that the other had not seen him. No doubt they were all wondering what he meant to do, whether he would back down at the last moment. Some of them would be expecting him to do just that, he thought grimly. If they did, then they were going to be sorely disappointed.

Going back to the bed, he stretched himself out on it, staring up at the ceiling. Was he doing the right thing? he wondered idly, stepping feet first into this trouble, this feud between Norma Holmes and Scott Kearney? To be quite truthful, it really was nothing to do with him and there had been little need for him to interfere as he had.

Minutes passed slowly. Outside, the dawn brightened quickly. The stars were no longer visible and shadows were long and huge in the street. Finally, he pushed himself upright, swung his legs to the floor and stretched himself, striving to ease, in some small way, the tension that still knotted itself in his mind and body.

Hitching the gunbelt a little higher around his middle, he glanced out of the window, looking along the street towards the stage depot. The stage was ready now, with the four horses in the traces, standing docilely enough in the growing light. The agent was talking earnestly with two men on the board-walk nearby, men dressed in black frock coats. There was a woman standing a little apart from them, her white poke bonnet showing clearly in the dawn light. So it was possible there would be passengers on this trip, after all. Maybe these people had to travel of necessity and even the thought that the stage might not get through had not been sufficient to deter them. As he watched, there was a movement along the boardwalk and a moment later, Norma Holmes came into view. He noticed at once that she was dressed for going away and almost without thinking, he turned and left the room, made his way down the creaking stairs and into the lobby. The clerk had evidently been waiting for him to appear for he called loudly:

'Mister Mannix. Could I have a word with you before you go?'

Cal halted, then turned back. 'Yes, what is it?' he asked tersely.

'We'd like to know if we're to keep the room for you, sir,' asked the other softly. His gaze gave nothing away and his expression was non-commital.

'I'll only be gone four days,' snapped Cal tightly. He glared at the other, knowing exactly what was in the man's mind.

'I agree that the return journey is only four days, Mister Mannix,' nodded the other smoothly. He seemed suddenly sure of himself. 'But that doesn't mean to say that you'll be back.'

Cal swallowed once as he felt the anger beginning to rise in him, but his tone was ice-steady as he replied: 'No need to worry about gettin' your money. I'll be back here to reclaim the room on Thursday night — with the stage intact. Anybody who thinks different had better watch himself.'

Straight-backed, he walked out of the hotel into the first glimmerings of sunlight. A small crowd had gathered and he caught a glimpse of the sheriff near the stage, talking with Norma Holmes. There was no sign of Scott Kearney and the fact troubled him a little. He would have felt easier in his mind if he knew he was here in town, and not out there someplace, roaming the hills along the trail he had to take. The sheriff placed his narrowed eyes on Cal as he went forward, then his glance dropped to the gunbelt around the other's middle and a new expression gusted over his features, a blend of fear and quick appraisal. There was a little murmur from the crowd too as they noticed the guns and Cal felt a moment's grim amusement at the way they turned to stare at each other.

'Everythin' ready'?' he asked of the agent.

The other nodded mutely, then caught himself and said harshly: 'All set to move out, mister. You've got four passengers on this trip. Tried to talk 'em out of it, but they seem determined to ride with you.'

'Five passengers.' Norma Holmes's voice reached him from somewhere in the crowd and a moment later, she pushed her way through them. Out of the corner of his eye, Cal caught the look on the sheriff's face at this remark, saw him fade back a little and then pause, disconcerted, as he felt Cal's gaze on him. He came forward again.

'Better keep a look out for trouble, mister,' he said tightly, striving to keep his tone even. 'There's been a mighty lot of trouble lately with this stageline and so far, we ain't managed to catch up with the outlaws who're doin' it.'

Cal nodded, but said nothing. Instead, he turned to the girl as the other passengers began to mount into the waiting coach. 'Are you sure that you have to travel on this stage, Norma?' he said in a harsh undertone. 'The others are safe enough. The outlaws want little from them except for the few valuables they might be carrying. But you're a different prospect altogether. They'd be able to finish off the two of us if you come along.'

'I've got business in Red Rock, Cal,' she said loudly, so that everyone in the crowd could hear. 'And I prefer to go by my own stage.'

'Suit yourself,' he said thinly. 'But I notice that Kearney ain't around to see us off and the sheriff is mighty anxious to get away as soon as he can to spread the word around.'

'All the more reason why I should come along.' She gave him a quick smile which warmed her face. 'I have to help protect my own interests, you know.'

There was no way of making her change her mind. Cal knew from past experience that once a woman of Norma's calibre made up her mind to do something, nothing on earth would make her alter it.

He helped her into the coach, then shut the door after her and moved around to the front, climbing up into the driver's seat. Glancing down, he let his gaze wander over the faces of the men and women in the crowd. One thing he noticed right away. Sometime during the few moments he had spent talking to the girl, the sheriff had seized his chance and slipped away. He lifted his head and stared back, over the roof of the coach, along the dusty street; but there was no sign of the other. The faint feeling of uneasiness grew within him. Events were crowding him, moving too quickly for him to take everything in at once and plan accordingly.

The agent gave him a quick grin, waved his right hand. Cracking the long lash of the whip, Cal started the horses moving along the street. The sun was just lifting over the desert as they drove out of town and took the long, snaking trail that led through the tall, pleasant trees. The sun had not yet risen sufficiently to bring the heat with it and the air was pleasant and cool against Cal's face as he stared out ahead of him, eyes wandering from side to side, still alert for trouble although it was highly unlikely that they would try to stop the stage so close to town. Snake Pass was the ideal spot for a hold up and there seemed little possibility of an attack much before then. Still, there was no call for him to be complacent. He remembered Norma Holmes, seated in the stage behind him and his uneasiness grew. Why had she persisted in riding with them when she knew there was sure to be trouble?

Within a mile, they moved out into the open again. After the first downward pitch of the trail, the road with its torturous windings levelled out and grew wider. The country around them spread out and Cal felt a sense of relief in his mind as he was able to see much further on all sides. The trees fell behind and he let the horses have their head. The sun lifted and the heat head increased in its dusty intensity. Thrown up by the pounding hoofs of the horses, the dust was everywhere. It penetrated the bandana he had pulled up over his mouth and nose, lay in a thick layer on the sides of the coach and entered through the partly open windows. Now that the full heat of the day was on them, the passengers in the coach had the choice of stewing in the heat, ovenlike and oppressive, or getting a little air about them, but having to put up with the dust.

He halted the team an hour later, letting the horses have a chance to blow. Far ahead of them, it was possible to make out where the trail lifted from the flat smoothness of the wide valley and crawled up the steep, rocky side of the foothills. Snake Pass was about fifteen miles or so further on, he guessed. Once again, the feeling of tension rose swiftly within him and he let his right hand drop by his side, touching the butt of the pistol in its leather holster. After so long, the guns felt heavy and awkward, but there was still the old familiar feel of them there, something he doubted if he would ever be able to forget.

'Why are we stopping here, driver?' called one of the frock-coated men, thrusting his head out of the window of the coach and staring up at him.

'Got to give the horses a chance to get their wind,' he called back. 'We've got one long drag ahead of us once we get into those hills yonder and they'll need all of their strength to haul this coach along that stretch of the trail.'

The answer evidently satisfied the other for he pulled his head inside again. Five minutes later, Cal cracked the whip over the sweating backs of the horses and they strained against the traces like one. The coach lurched forward with a creaking of steelbound wooden wheels, springs straining as they began to climb. There was a stretch of dangerous trail and the horses picked their way forward carefully until they had reached the end of it. From that point on the going was rough, but easier than before and they made good time, moving upgrade all the time. The minutes passed and each one brought them nearer Snake Pass and with the sun almost at its zenith and glaring straight in his eyes, Cal knew that he would be at a distinct disadvantage when they did strike. But he had chosen the path he was to take, and he had to go through with it now.

They turned the cliff's gradual bend, the coach swaying violently from side to side. Down to their left, the trail dropped away suddenly for a sheer three hundred feet into a loose slide of boulders at the very bottom of the slope. But it was evident that the horses knew every inch of this trail and although the off-side wheels were less than a foot from the edge of the trail,

Cal had little worry about them going over the side. On the right, there was a massive wall of rock which almost shut out the sun so that for part of the way they drove in shadow, but with the yellow dust still riding with them.

Familiar landmarks showed up now, remembered from his journey here the previous day and he found himself watching for them to appear on either side of the trail, enabling him to judge exactly where he was. Whenever he could, he glanced up towards rough breaks in the rock wall on his right, scanning the undulating skyline for any sign of trouble, any indication that their progress was being followed by men along a higher trail than that which they rode.

They reached a narrow stream half an hour later, the clear water bubbling swiftly down the slope from the crests of the tall mountains. It had been born there, high up, would wind its way down the slope until it wandered into a wider river somewhere out on the plains. But here, the bottom was stone, the water cool and crystal clear and he halted the team in the middle of it, letting the horses drink while he sat tall in the seat, stretching himself to ease a little of the cramp which threatened to knot his muscles, while he scanned the territory around them. From this point it was possible to make out the rocks and chasms that lay within five or six miles of them. As far as the eye could see, nothing moved. There was no tell-tale glint of sunlight striking metal that would warn him of the presence of drygulchers hidden in the rocks ahead, waiting for them to draw level with their hiding place.

Rolling himself a smoke, he leaned his shoulders back and relaxed. The Winchester in its leather scabbard was loaded and ready for instant use should it be needed. He had checked that point before they had pulled out of Sherman City. His mouth was dry and the smoke from the cigarette gave him little pleasure. Bending from his perch on the seat, he lowered his head so that he was able to peer inside the coach.

'If any of you gentlemen would care to get rid of some of the dust, I can recommend the water in the stream,' he suggested.

The suggestion was received with vague shakes of the head. He noticed Norma glancing up at him, and saw the lines of strain and worry that showed quite clearly on her regular features. After a few moments, she said softly: 'Where are we now, Cal?'

'About four miles from Snake Pass.' He spoke lightly but deliberately, knowing the thoughts which must have been going through her mind at that moment. 'Once we're through there, we leave the mountains behind and head out over the desert. We stop the night at the way station there. The agent will make you all quite comfortable, but we'll be miles from anywhere, so I hope none of you mind listening to nothin' but the coyotes at night.'

'I'm quite sure I won't sleep a wink,'

said one of the women, a vague look of horror on her face. 'But I suppose anything would be preferable to remaining in this coach with the heat and the dust everywhere.'

'We'll be movin' on in a couple of minutes, Ma'am,' he said easily. 'Just givin' the horses a breather. Unlikely they'll get any more water until we hit the way station around nightfall.'

The going was tough now. The trail led upgrade and the slope was far sharper, far steeper, than Cal had remembered it from the last trip. The horses strained against creaking leather, thrusting onward with every ounce of strength in their bodies, sweat running in rivulets down their heaving flanks. Rocks studded the slope and long before they reached Snake Pass, they were forced to move at a crawl. Any chance of rushing the Pass and gaining the comparative safety of the stretching desert on the other side, was gone, Cal thought grimly. He tried to watch the ground on either side of the trail now, where the rocks had closed in about them. Dust hung thick and heavy and yellow in the air and the heat of the day was on them. Once, glancing down so that he could see Norma Holmes's face at the window of the coach, he had caught the fleeting smile she gave him, and a feeling of deep admiration for her flooded through him at that moment. Close on its heels came anger at men like Kearney and that crooked sheriff, men to whom money meant everything, meant more than upholding the law and protecting innocent men and women.

The girl, at the moment, was actually more afraid for him than for herself. She knew that it was here that any attack on the coach would take place and it had never entered her head that, even if the outlaws were working in league with the sheriff and Scott Kearney, they would wish to harm her. Certainly, she did not doubt that they would do everything in their power to get the stageline from her, whether it was by legal means or otherwise. But there was no necessity for them to kill her. On the other hand, Cal Mannix had shown up Scott in town, and in front of some of the townsfolk, and she knew from past experience that Scott's pride would not allow that to go unpunished.

She leaned her shoulders back against the back of her seat and peered intently through the windows, striving to make out any movement in the rocks on that side of the trail. It was difficult to see anything. The dust that had been kicked up during the past few hours had laid a thick layer of yellow on the outside of the windows and the strong sunlight, refracted off this layer, hazed everything so that she was able to make out only scant details of their surroundings.

Turning her attention away for a while, she eyed the faces of her companions. In the far corner, one of the men had fallen asleep, his mouth hanging open a little, his head lolling forward on his chest. The other man was staring through the opposite window, watching the rugged scenery idly. None of the four passengers seemed aware of the possibility of any danger to the coach at this point. She felt a little wave of thankfulness for that. People such as these tended to panic at the first sign of trouble instead of keeping their heads, and outlaws such as those who operated in these hills were inclined to do mean things to anyone who either panicked or tried to hide any valuables they might be carrying.

Glancing back out of the window, she saw that they were almost at the top of the incline. The narrow pass through the rocks loomed ahead of them, only a couple of hundred yards away. Still no sign of trouble. At any moment, she expected to hear the sharp bark of a rifle warning them to stop and the harsh voice of one of the outlaws commanding them to step out of the coach. Would Cal carry out his threat and attempt to fight them, she wondered. Had there been another man up there with him, it was possible, but no man could drive a coach and fire a rifle at the same time. Besides, it was difficult getting a stage through that narrow pass yonder at the best of times. There had been many occasions when Clem had claimed that only a coat of paint lay between the coach and the looming rock on either side.

On the driver's seat, his feet braced against the wooden crossbar, hands holding tightly on to the reins, Cal felt the tension beginning to rise more swiftly and commandingly now. Everything around them seemed still and menacing. Too still; too quiet. Swiftly, he scanned the rising rocks on either side of the trail for the last time before they moved into the pass, saw nothing, then was forced to concentrate all of his attention on guiding the horses through. The rocky walls of the canyon closed in on them swiftly, rushing at them from both sides and the creaking echoes of the wheels were thrown back from the rocks until they boomed in his ears.

Three minutes elapsed before they broke out of the Pass and came out into the flooding yellow sunlight again. Cal blinked his eyes rapidly several times, adjusting them quickly to the glare, every nerve stretched taut within him. It seemed incredible that they had succeeded in getting through the pass without any trouble. Had something happened about which he knew nothing? Had the sheriff been riding out of town to warn the outlaws that Norma Holmes was riding the stage with them and that Kearney did not want her hurt? It was only a vague possibility. He doubted if these men had any feelings. One of the horses snorted softly and his gaze darted swiftly to one side, seeking the reason. Something must have spooked the animal, but there was nothing in sight. With his left hand, he lifted the Winchester from its scabbard and held it carefully in his hand, his fingers tight across the trigger. At first, he could see nothing. Then the indistinct shape of a man appeared, moving from shadow to shadow some forty feet from the edge of the trail, weaving from side to side. Cal held his breath for a moment, watching the man approach.

Some kind of trap? Was the man there to hold his attention while the rest of the outlaw band sneaked up on him from some other direction? He swung his gaze away momentarily, then glanced back when he saw nothing suspicious.

Then he heard Norma's excited voice calling from the window of the coach. 'That man there, Cal. He's been hurt!'

For perhaps ten seconds there was complete silence. Then Cal reined up the horses, pulled on the brake and dropped lightly to the ground, moving up into the rocks, still clutching the rifle in his right hand, eyes alert for the first sign of danger. It was as he clambered over a low ledge that he picked out the starved echo in the distance, far away and moving still further from them. The dull beat of horses drumming over rocks. He listened to it with a part of his mind until it had faded completely and he could hear it no longer. Stunted trees thrust themselves up from the sparse soil, dragging what little moisture they could from the stony ground. Very little could grow here amid the rocks and boulders. The soil was only dust, dried by the sun to a fine powder. It had no depth, could not retain the moisture for long.

As he moved forward, he held himself close to the ground, still not sure whether he would draw a shot from somewhere above him. Then he crawled out of the shallow canyon into a stretch of open ground. The man he had seen a few moments earlier lay sprawled a few yards away in the shade of a thick bush. Cal hurried forward, went down on one knee beside the other, turned him over gently. His face was chalk white and there was a thin smear of blood on his cheek, but in spite of this, Cal recognized him at once. The man he had met up with the previous day when he had been riding these hills, the man who seemed to have been running away from trouble. Now, trouble had caught up with him again, bad trouble.

The man opened his eyes, stared up at Cal for a long moment, not really seeing him. He said through clenched teeth: 'Yuh come back to see me off, killer?'

Cal shook his head slowly, pillowed the man's head. 'You'll be all right when we get you to a doctor.'

'Finished now ... no use gettin' doctor for me.' A spasm of pain lanced through his body and his back arched a little, then relaxed abruptly. Sweat popped out on his forehead and his lips were thinned back over his teeth.

'You see who shot you?'

'Shot me down from cover. Bush-whacked me up yonder near the mountain trail. Fifteen or twenty of 'em, I reckon.'

Cal nodded grimly. The man was about cashed. He must have known himself that he had only a few more minutes to live. The slugs in him must have cut into his lungs, probably nicked his heart. It was a miracle that he was still alive. But he had given Cal the clue to the identity of his killers. Somehow, somewhere, he had run foul of that outlaw band and they had given him short shrift. The old ways of violence, never changing and never different, working their way through this part of the territory and in this little stretch of time. Maybe in another ten, twenty, years, there would be nothing of this and these outlaws would have been wiped out and law and order established permanently, even here. But these were the times in which they were forcd to live and one had to meet violence with violence, merely to stay alive.

'Yuh ridin' out after that bunch?' Somehow, the dying man forced the words through shaking lips.

'Sure. I'll get 'em if it's the last thing I do.' Cal knew that he lied, but there was nothing else he could do.

The man's body arched once more as he coughed, a horrible, bubbling cough that brought flecks of blood to his mouth. But the racking spasm, bringing the deepseated agony with it, brought consciousness back fully into his pain-twisted mind and he looked up at Cal with a measure in his eyes. 'Say, yuh're the stranger rode into my camp yesterday and — ' His voice broke off, his lips worked slackly for a long moment while the wheezing sounds continued at the back of his throat.

'Take it easy, mister,' said Cal softly. 'I can't do much for you at the moment and it's — '

The man's head rolled awkwardly on his skinny neck as if he were struggling desperately to regain the strength of his muscles. Once more his lips worked spasmodically, but no words came out and his right hand, which he had somehow lifted to clutch at Cal's sleeve,

161

merely rested there as though he had no strength to lift it again.

'You know where that gang was headed?'

Even in his badly-wounded state, the dying man looked surprised at that question. Then he nodded, still unable to speak. His eyes asked how Cal knew of the outlaws as he tried to focus them on the other. The muscles of his neck corded for a moment as he strove to give voice to his thoughts.

'Desert! Desert trail!' The words coughed out of him, sending him into a racking spasm once more. The effort to speak must have increased the internal haemorrhage for he suddenly clutched at Cal's shirt, fingers digging in with the last ounce of his strength, a convulsive movement, fingers clawed.

'They've ridden out into the desert? They haven't stayed here near Snake Pass?' Cal asked the questions urgently, knowing instinctively that there was little time left.

The other's lips twisted back into a

faint affirmative smile at his words and he tried to nod, but it was as if he could no longer control any of the muscles in his body. Giving a last, final wheeze, his head fell sideways and his whole body relaxed. Carefully, Cal laid him down on the hard ground, got stiffly to his feet and stood looking down at the other for a moment. Even though he was dead, there was still that faint suggestion of a smile on his lips, as if the man had died happy, knowing that he had given information to Cal which should enable him to catch up with the men who had killed him.

Quickly, Cal made his way back to the coach. If the dead man had told the truth, they had nothing to fear here, but he knew he would not feel easier in his mind until they were out of these hills and rocks and into the stretching wilderness of the desert and on their way on the last stage of the journey to the way station.

Norma Holmes had got out of the coach and was standing by the side of the trail, waiting for him. She gave him an apprehensive glance as he came up to her.

He forced a quick smile, but it was a grim expression with no mirth in it. 'The man I ran into yesterday. He must have bumped into the outlaws. They shot him and left him there to die.'

'He's dead then?'

'Yes, he's dead. Nothin' I could do for him. Shot through the chest from close range. They must've bushwhacked him from the rocks.' He urged her back into the coach and closed the door after her, anxious to be moving out.

'Did he tell you anything?' she asked as he moved away.

Turning, he nodded slowly, aware that the other passengers were watching him closely, no doubt listening to every word that was said. 'He reckoned that those others were headed out into the desert.'

'Do you think he was right?'

'I'm not sure.' Cal tightened his lips into a hard, determined line as he climbed up on to the seat, thrusting the Winchester back into its scabbard. 'He may have been mistaken. It ain't the sort of thing I'd have expected 'em to do. There ain't no place out there where they can attack us without givin' plenty of warning of their presence.'

He cracked the long whip over the backs of the horses. Very slowly, creaking in every spring, the stage moved off, over the crest of the hill and then down the winding trail that led out across the desert, now clearly seen in front of them. At a steady pace, they rode over the rough ground where the rocks petered out, cutting into the desert country, the badlands. There were no signs along the trail that a bunch of men had ridden this way recently. Either the badly wounded man had been wrong, confused; or the outlaws had kept well clear of the trail, skirting it somewhere to the north so as not to give away their presence. They would not have banked on the dying man being still alive when Cal had found him, and giving away their plans before he died.

The sun had lifted now until it was right at the zenith, burning in the cloudless blue heavens, laying a scorching touch on his neck and shoulders. The metalwork of the bridles flashed lances of fire into his eyes. It was a terrible trail, one which was used almost exclusively by the stage, since to compete with the railroad, they had to take the shortest possible route between Sherman City and Red Rock. He watched constantly, ahead, each side, back in the direction from which they had just come. In places, the trail dipped down almost to the point where it crowded into the buttes and then again, it would angle steeply, high up the side of the deep canyons, around steep, dangerous bends to skirt the meandering sandstone walls of the bluffs.

By the time they had travelled for three hours over the desert, and the sun was beginning to wester, still burning with a vicious heat, every dusty, heat-seared fibre and nerve in his body had set up a mocking scream deep within him. In front of him, the trail stretched endlessly towards the buttes that rose up on the horizon, and in between, still to be crossed before nightfall, was a terrible land of alkali and scrub. Slitting his eyes against the terrible, fierce glare of the sun, he scanned the empty plain that lay in front of him, a vast wilderness from which the searing heat of the sun seemed to have taken all of the colour. He could see nothing. There was no sign of any riders there, no indication that the outlaws were anywhere ahead of them.

The stage rattled down a treacherous slope, bouncing and swaying from side to side. Few springs gushed up in this ugly country and the ground was arid and inhospitable, dotted only by the green-brown scrub, a few cacti that stood like silent sentinels all about them, the only vegetation to be seen.

Sand and sweat worked its way into the folds of his skin, filling them with an itching ache that was both painful and irritating. The horses plodded steadily forward now, heads down, the sun beating down on them, almost blinding them. There was no shade here, no place to escape the fiery, pitiless glare of the sun. Cal rode in silence, speculating. As yet, he had no plan to put into action, if and when the outlaws did attack. That was a bridge he would have to cross when he came to it, he decided inwardly. There was no sense in filling his mind with problems now, slowing his reflexes down to danger point.

Half an hour later, he halted the horses in a sandy cut that ran at right angles to the main trail, beside a gummy water hole. The sunglow that filled the overhead dust was a sickening glare and the heat waves seemed to be refracted from every part of the desert, beating in endless waves against his face. Even the air felt as if it had been drawn through some gigantic oven before it reached them. Glancing up, he noticed there were a few buzzards wheeling like tattered strips of black cloth against the sky.

'Anybody care to alight for a spell?' he asked, getting down and holding open the door of the coach.

One by one, all of the passengers climbed out, stood in a little group and looked about them at their surroundings. One of the men took a gold watch from the pocket of his waistcoat and glanced at it meaningly. Then he looked up at Cal. 'You still reckon we'll reach that way station by sundown, mister?' he asked tightly.

'I reckon so,' Cal replied evenly. 'Another ten miles to go. Then there ought to be food waitin' for us and a bed for the night. Tomorrow, we'll be on our way into Red Rock.'

'Maybe we should have taken the train,' suggested one of the women, a pretty, fragile thing, glancing up at the man.

'Perhaps,' grunted the other. He

pursed his lips tightly, glanced down at the water that showed at the bottom of the mud-hole. 'We don't have to drink that filth, do we?'

'Plenty of fresh water in the barrel at the back,' Cal nodded towards the rear of the coach. 'Help yourself.'

The man grunted something under his breath, then moved around to the rear of the stage, took the small tin mug from its hook and drew off some of the water, tasted it with a grimace. 'This water is hot,' he complained.

Cal lifted his brows. There was a faint feeling of irritation stirring in him, as he retorted. 'Ought to be, mister, seein' as how it's been out in the sun most of the journey.'

Surlily, the man finished his drink, poured what was left in the mug on to the sand and hung it up on the hook again. Cal went over to him, grinning tightly. 'Seems to me you ain't been in this part of the territory long, mister,' he said with an ominous softness.

The man ought to have recognized

the danger signal, but he did not; 'Just what do you mean by that remark, friend?' he asked thickly.

'Out here, when we have to travel over the desert, we don't waste water; not even a drop. No tellin' when you're goin' to need it. Only a fool pours it away like you did just then.'

For a moment, the other squared up to him, his face purpling a little. His eyes slitted angrily. 'I don't like your tone, mister,' he snapped. 'I paid my fare to travel on this stage and if I want to pour half of my drink on to the sand, then by God, I intend to do it.'

Cal clenched his fist by his side. 'Reckon you do have that right,' he said quietly.

The other nodded, evidently satisfied. 'So long as you recognize that fact, I don't mind,' he said.

'But I ought to point out to you, that if we ever get into a spot when we have to ration what little water we have, you'll be forced to go without by the same amount that you've wasted.'

'There's no question of such an occasion arising.' The other did not seem quite as sure of himself. 'You said youself a few moments ago that it was only a matter of ten miles to the way station where we'll get plenty of food and drink and it seems to me that the trail is clearly marked. No possibility of us losing our way, even in the dark.'

In answer, Cal pointed to the wheeling buzzards overhead. 'There are buzzards and coyotes out here in the desert, and men with the habits of both. This stage has been held up by outlaws on several occasions during the past few weeks. We were lucky back there at Snake Pass. That's their favourite jumpin' place. But that don't mean to say we're out of danger yet. The man I found in the rocks had been shot down by outlaws who'd left him there to die. But he told me that these men had taken the desert trail. They could be out here watchin' us right now. They know we have to come this way.'

'Outlaws!' uttered one of the women.

'But they told us in town that the sheriff had ridden out with a posse to hunt these men down. That we had nothing to worry about on this trip.'

'Who told you that?' asked Cal abruptly.

'Why Mister Kearney. He seemed so sure about it all.'

Cal said softly: 'I've no doubt he thought it would be all right.' He walked back to the coach, motioned them all inside again. Helping up the girl, he felt her lean a little against him, felt the warmth of her body against his. Raising his eyes, he saw the smile that touched her lips. Then she had taken her seat again, leaning back in the coach. He clambered up slowly into the driver's seat, brushed the sleeve of his jacket across his face to wipe the sweat from his eyes. His eyes were smeared with the yellow dust. He tasted it on his lips and took a quick drink from his canteen, swilling the warm, brackish water around his mouth for a moment, before swallowing it.

At seven o'clock, the country lifted a little from its flatness. He saw that they had reached the buttes which he had noticed earlier and there were rolling dunes of sand and clay gulches all about them; with here and there a pine tree that lifted solitary and alone, standing out darkly against the blue sky. To the west, the sky flamed with the sunset. Deep reds and oranges lay over the dimpled horizon and although the sun itself could no longer be seen, there were still the signs of it over the rim of the world, a last great burst of flame. After that, the reds and scarlets faded swiftly and it became a deep blue world, with a lessening of the intense heat that had been with them ever since they had ridden up into the rocks west of Snake Pass. Cal felt the coolness that flowed against him and straightened a little in the seat, feeling the aches in his body that came from sitting too long in the same position. He stretched his legs out straight in front of him to ease the pincers of cramp that shot through the long muscles of his thighs.

Half an hour later, with the stars just beginning to show, and the moon lifting over the eastern horizon, round and huge, they came within sight of the way station, with the cluster of trees around it and the wide corral, staked off from the rest of the ground. The pounding hoofs of the horses sounded hollowly in the small courtyard as they drove in, halting in front of the long, low-roofed house.

Thankfully, he clambered down from his perch, letting the reins fall over the backs of the horses. Opening the door of the stage, he helped the three women down, then stood on one side as the two men alighted.

'So we finally made it,' grunted the taller of the two men. He looked about him with a sudden interest. 'Is this the station?'

'That's right.' Cal nodded as he closed the stage door. 'This is all there is to it and I reckon I ought to point out that we're miles from anywhere out here. The only company you'll get are the coyotes.'

The agent drifted out of the shadows of the long building, took the horses and nodded towards the open door. 'Go along inside, folks,' he called. 'I'll be with you in a couple of minutes, as soon as I've put the stage away and turned the horses loose in the corral.'

Cal followed the others into the building. There was a fire blazing in a wide hearth and he judged that the nights here were inclined to be on the cold side. The women moved over to the fire. Rolling himself a smoke, Cal went over to the bar at the far side of the room, reached over the counter and pulled out a bottle and a couple of glasses, glanced round at the two men nearby. They were watching him with an equal interest and after a brief pause, they came over, resting their elbows on the counter. Cal poured them out a drink, then one for himself.

'I reckon this should wash the dust of the journey off your tonsils, gentlemen,' he said quietly. He swallowed the liquor in a single gulp. The whiskey went down into his stomach and exploded in a haze of warmth. Suddenly, he felt fine, with a fresh current of interest running through him. At least, they had reached their first objective without too much trouble. The rest of the journey into Red Rock should prove to be equally uneventful.

The agent returned, closed the door and locked it, pushing the wooden bar into place. He gave Cal a head-on glance as he moved behind the bar. 'Why ain't Clem with the stage? Anythin' happened?'

'He stopped a slug in the shoulder on the last trip.'

'Outlaws?'

Cal nodded. 'That's right. Seems they're tryin' to stop the stage gettin' through. Then according to the contract, Miss Holmes loses the line.'

'That why she's here with yuh?'

'Guess so. She insisted on comin' along for the ride and nothin' I could say would stop her.'

'She's that kind of woman,' agreed the other. He took a cloth and wiped the top of the counter. 'That's how she must've kept this stageline runnin' when everythin' seemed to be agin her.' He broke off. 'Reckon I'd better get the supper ready. Yuh must all be starvin' after that long drive.'

* * *

Cal was glad when the food came. The smoke had tasted bad in his mouth, and on his empty stomach. It had been a long, hard day and the food tasted good, far better than he had expected. When he had finished, he got to his feet and moved over to the door. Reaching up, he was on the point of taking down the wooden bar when the agent stopped him.

'Reckon it might be best not to touch that, Cal,' he said quietly.

Something in the other's tone made Cal turn quickly and he scanned the old man's face intently. 'Somethin' wrong?' he asked quietly. 'You're not usually as edgy as this.'

'I'm not sure.' The other's voice was urgent enough to make Cal restless, and he could not shake off his sudden suspicion.

'Well, speak up, man. What was it?' He gave the other a hard stare. 'You must've seen or heard somethin' to make you act like this.'

'Mebbe it was nothin',' muttered the other. 'But I reckoned I heard riders movin' close to the station earlier this afternoon.'

'Did you see anythin'?'

'Nope. Unless yuh call the suspicion of a dust cloud somethin' definite. I'm sure I weren't imaginin' anythin'.'

'I'm sure you weren't.' He related quickly about the finding of the dying man among the rocks near Snake Pass. When he had finished, the agent nodded his head quickly. 'Makes sense. They might ride this way, try to sneak upon us when it's dark.'

'I'm goin' out to take a look around.'

'Take care. They may be out there now,' warned the other harshly. 'If they left their mounts out among the trees, we would never have heard 'em.'

'I'll keep my eyes open,' Cal turned. 'Better douse that lantern.'

The agent moved away, extinguished the lamp. Quietly, Cal opened the door and stepped through, closing it softly behind him. For a moment, he stood there with his back against the wall, searching about him with his eyes and ears. The out-buildings were silent mounds of shadow with the pale moonlight lying over the wide corral. Hesitating only for a few seconds, he jerked one of the guns from its holster, then edged forward, an inch at a time. The feeling of danger was strong in him although he could see and hear nothing. Then one of the horses in the corral suddenly snickered, the faint murmur of sound carrying clearly in the silence. Instinctively, he thrust himself back against the wall, crowding

180

the shadows. Something had spooked that horse, something in the shadows of the trees on the far edge of the corral.

There was a blank, intense silence for a few seconds and in the corral, the horses were now peaceable enough. He had been mistaken? Crouching down, he edged out into the open, moved forward until he was down below the wooden fencing around the corral. There were deep black shadows among the trees, shadows thrown by the moonlight, shadows where twenty or thirty men could hide, without being seen from the way station.

Then, through the silence, a sound came and grew. There was a cracking of twigs among the trees as several men moved forward towards the far side of the corral. One of the horses near that side was obviously nervous. It began to shy away from the fence, then moved away into the middle of the open space. Grasping the Colt tightly in his fist, Cal watched the fringe of trees, moving his gaze slowly from side to side. Several seconds passed, then he caught a glimpse of the dark shadow that flitted from one concealing clump of darkness to another. In the moonlight it was difficult to see the man properly, but this was no ordinary caller.

Cal's mouth was a tight thin line as he listened. There was a sudden muttering of voices among the trees. Then two more shapes moved out into the open and began to work their way cautiously around the fence, moving towards the station building. He could not afford to let them come any closer. His first shot would warn those in the station. It would also warn those men out there, but that was a risk he had to take. Squinting along the sights, he drew a bead on one of the men, squeezed the trigger. The gun bucked against his wrist and the blast of the shot echoed and bucketed through the clinging stillness. The man stumbled forward, hands clutching at his chest. Then he toppled out of sight.

The other man, moving behind the

dead man, suddenly let out an ear-splitting yell of warning and went for his gun. Cal loosed off a couple of shots and then ducked back out of sight. A bullet crashed into the wooden fence above his head, chewed a large sliver out of it and then ricocheted off into the darkness. Guns roared again and again, flames tulipping out of the darkness. Cal noticed that the outlaws had swung around until they had almost surrounded the way station. More slugs hummed like a swarm of angry hornets about him as he turned and darted back towards the house. He could hear them hammering on the walls. There was a crash of breaking glass as one of the windows was shattered and he distinctly heard a thin, high-pitched scream from one of the women in the station house. There were loud yells from behind him and throwing a swift glance over his shoulder, he caught sight of the rest of the outlaws running across the corral. He snaked a couple of shots at them, saw one of them go down under the plunging hoofs of one of the horses.

Moments later, he reached the door, thrust it open, slamming it behind him. The agent came running forward from behind the bar, clutching an old-fashioned rifle in his hands. He took up his position by one of the windows. Norma Holmes ran over to the lantern which had been relit. The room was plunged into darkness. Outside, guns were blasting and he heard a harsh voice roaring orders.

'You see who they were?' asked one of the men harshly.

'Nope,' Cal shook his head. 'But I can guess. They're the men I expected to attack the stage back at Snake Pass.' Crouched by the window, he peered out into the moonlit darkness. He had a couple of the men located. The fellows were out there some twenty yards away, faint blurs at the edge of the livery stable. Cal weighed his chances of hitting them from that distance. A gun spiked flame from one of the men and the slug tore into the wooden uprights of the window. He flinched instinctively, then brought up his own weapon, swept the barrel into line and squeezed off a couple of shots, both of which found their targets. There came the sound of a muffled cry, a savage curse, and then a floundering over the uneven ground. One man lay where he had fallen, unmoving in the moonlight. The other staggered away, one arm clutching at the wooden rails of the corral for support and then slumped down before he could reach cover. Cal drove another shot at him, saw the man's body twitch and then lie still.

'Fine shootin', son,' grunted the agent. He lifted the rifle as a bunch of men came rushing out of the darkness. The blast almost deafened Cal, the sound reverberating in the confined space of the room. Three men threw up their arms and fell in huddled heaps. The others hesitated, then dived back under cover, not liking the chance they had of reaching the house alive.

There was a pause in the firing, while Cal reloaded the chambers of his guns. He squinted through the smashed window, trying to pick out anything that moved, but the outlaws had fallen back into the trees. At least five of them had been killed in that attempt to rush the station house. But there were twenty or thirty more of them out there and Cal was the first to recognize the precariousness of their plight.

'Yuh figger they'll try to rush us again, after that dose o' lead we just gave 'em?' asked the agent.

'They'll come. But they'll take their time. They know we can't make a break for it from here. They've got the entire place surrounded. Besides, even if we did manage to get out of the house unseen, we'd never manage to get one of the horses from the corral from under their noses.'

'God damn it, Cal — you reckon they mean to sit there and starve us out?'

Cal pondered that possibility for a

brief moment, then rejected it, shaking his head. 'We've got plenty of grub and water too. They know they can't starve us out of here. Besides, when the stage doesn't reach Red Rock, they'll send some men out to check what happened to us within a couple of days. Nope, I figure they mean to crowd us as soon as they git the chance.'

'Mebbe we could sneak out before it's light and get one o' them horses,' suggested the other tightly.

'Not a chance. They'll be watchin' the corral, just waitin' for the chance to pot us.'

'Then what do you think we can do?' broke in one of the other men. He stood over by the far side of the room, his back against the bar and Cal noticed that he had made certain he was not in the line of fire from any of the windows.

'If you think of anythin' that might help us, I'd be glad if you'd let the rest of us know,' said Cal tightly. He turned back to the window in time to see two men move towards one of the barns.

The darkness rocked to the rhythm of death as Cal triggered back the hammers of his guns with his thumbs, the sounds of his shots blending with the roaring blasts from the agent's rifle. He could hear the hot lead from the outlaws' guns smashing into the walls and splintering the window frame. The outlaws were closing in tightly, firing as they came.

Then there was a sudden, inexplicable lull in the firing. Cal pressed himself tightly against the wall beside the window, trying to see out in the darkness. He gripped the Colts in his fists and waited, trying to figure out what might be happening outside.

Then a hoarse voice yelled: 'Yuh ain't got a chance, any of yuh. Step outside with yore hands raised and yuh won't get hurt.'

'Lyin' varmints,' grunted the agent from the other window. 'They'll shoot us down soon as we step through that door.'

'Maybe they won't,' muttered one of

the men, crouched down on the floor by the bar. 'If we give them any money and valuables we have, they may let us go free.'

'Yuh goin' to come out — or do we have to come in and git yuh?'

Cal edged forward an inch. 'We don't make deals with killers,' he called.

The silence lasted for a couple of seconds longer, then the darkness erupted flame as the guns opened up once more. A gun roared less than twenty feet away, close to the barn, the bullet only head high. Only the reflex crouch he made saved Cal then. Swiftly, he slammed a bullet in the direction of the hidden marksman, cursed himself roundly for not having realized that during the short palaver with the outlaw leader, his men had taken the opportunity to move forward in the dimness.

Over his shoulder, Cal said to the agent. 'You got the telegraph here, ain't you?'

'By golly, yuh're right. I'd clear forgot

about that. We can send a message through to Red Rock and have the sheriff and his posse out here before mornin'.'

Out of the corner of his eye, Cal saw the other lower his rifle and edge away into the room, keeping his head low. A moment later, someone else moved up beside him, and turning his head quickly, he saw Norma Holmes, crouching down beside him, saw that she held the Winchester which he had brought in from the stage.

'Keep your head down, Norma,' he whispered harshly. 'This is no work for a woman.'

'Those men out there are trying to take the stageline from me, the line my father worked and died for.' There was a quiet, savage intensity in her voice as she spoke. 'And I intend to stop them. We'll need every one who can handle a gun if we are to get out of this alive.'

Thumbing shells into his guns, he yelled at the others crouched down on the floor. 'If any of you value your lives,

I reckon you'd better grab a gun and help. Those *hombres* out there mean business and they won't leave any witnesses if they do manage to get in here. The women-folk can get down on the floor behind the bar where they should be safe.'

'Now see here,' began one of the men hoarsely. 'This fight is none of our business. We paid to get through to Red Rock and that means you were to protect us too.'

'That's just what I'm tryin' to do,' snapped Cal angrily. 'But it ain't possible for me to watch every side of the building. Now grab a couple of guns and head through into the back room, keep watch there. If you see anythin' moving' out in the yard, shoot to kill. You won't get a second chance.'

For a moment, he thought they meant to refuse. Perhaps it was the sight of Norma Holmes, standing by the window with the rifle grasped tightly and with determination in her hands, that finally decided them, or the

191

grim look on Cal's features as he faced them squarely. Scrambling to their feet, they moved around the bar, picked a couple of guns and some shells from the case at the back of the room and went out through the door.

The agent came back, his face grim. Gripping the old-fashioned rifle, he went back to the window, stood quickly to one side as a slug hummed through the glass and buried itself in the opposite wall.

'Well?' hissed Cal, 'did you get through to Red Rock?'

'Not a chance. The line's completely dead. Reckon those critters out there know their business. Must've cut the wires somewhere out in the desert.'

Cal's only answer to that was a grim nod. Those *hombres* seemed to have thought of everything. He peered through the window. Everything was ominously quiet and it was as if the outlaws had pulled back into the trees near the corral, not wishing to lose any more men, knowing that they had everybody holed up and that none of them could possibly escape without being seen and gunned down.

'Are they still there?' asked the girl softly.

'Among the trees. Maybe waitin' for us to make a run for it. I figured they might have been in a hurry to finish us, but if they've cut the telegraph wires, then they don't have to try to rush us before dawn. They can squat out yonder and keep us holed up here until they decide what to do with us.'

Standing by the window, his ears sucking in all of the sounds of the night outside, Cal felt the deep weariness in his body. His thinking was a trifle sluggish as he turned over in his mind all of the details he remembered of the terrain around the way station. For more than fifteen miles in every direction, there was only the desert and then the hills before one reached Red Rock. Even to try to reach the railroad would be a tremendous task and with the rest of the people here, they might never make it unless he could get the stage ready and hitch up the other team. He moved stiffly away from the window, thrusting the guns back into their holsters. The agent remained on watch, staring out into the moonlight.

Norma came over and stood beside him, her hand on his arm. Her face was troubled as she glanced up at him, but with an effort, she managed to give him a wan smile.

'We don't have much chance, do we?' she asked. Before he could speak, she went on quickly. 'Don't try to make things seem better than they are just to make it easier for me. There must be thirty men out there, waiting to kill us and even in daylight, it's doubtful if we could get out to the stage or the horses.'

Wearily, he sat down at the table, trying to relax, but knowing that it was impossible. The realization came to him then that with the wires cut, it might be days before anybody in Red Rock or Sherman City decided to come and look for them.

5

The Long Desert

'Somethin' happenin' out there,' called the agent sharply. Cal was on his feet in a moment, moving forward warily. He crouched down beside the other as he motioned the girl back when she made to follow him. Cautiously, he lifted his head to peer above the ledge of the window. At first, he could see nothing in the moonthrown shadows. One of the slain outlaws lay in a huddled heap by the edge of the corral and a little further away, the dead man's companion was hanging half over the lowermost stretch of the wooden fence.

Then he spotted the man who came out of the blackness of the trees in the distance, ran forward, doubled over, and threw himself down behind the barn. He held something in his right hand, but Cal could not make out what it was. Now that trouble seemed about to begin again, his mind was suddenly very clear, very sharp. He seemed to hear every sound as if it had been magnified, the movement of the horses in the corral, the sigh of the wind in the branches of the trees.

'What d'yuh reckon he's doin' back there?' grunted the agent, straightening his back a little. 'If he reckons on shootin' into the room from yonder, he'll have tuh expose himself to our fire. Must be that he means to — '

'Yuh comin' out with yore hands lifted, or do we kill yuh all?' called the same hoarse voice, yelling from the direction of the trees.

Instinctively, Cal switched his gaze from the barn where the running man had disappeared towards the sound of the voice. He tried to make out shapes among the trees but the flooding moonlight played tricks with a man's eyes and made him see things that were not really there. Moments later, he realized why the man had shouted at that particular moment, simply to distract their attention from the man behind the barn. He must have been carrying a torch of brush in his hands when he had made that sudden dash across the courtyard. The flare of red-tongued flame showed clearly once the straw in the barn caught. There were tiny tendrils of smoke lifting into the clear air and seconds later, Cal heard the vicious crackling as the fire took a firm hold.

'Hell, they've fired the barn,' called the agent. He turned to stare at Cal and there was a look of apprehension on his grizzled features. 'An' the wind is in the right direction to carry it to the station.'

Cal nodded grimly. The other was right. What wind there was would blow the flames and sparks in their direction once that fire really got a firm hold. He slitted his eyes against the darkness. Already, it was licking around the side of the barn, beginning to leap fiercely up the further wall. In the near distance, he could hear the frightened whinneying of the horses in the corral as they smelled the smoke.

'There's the sneakin' varmint,' roared the agent. Bringing the rifle to his shoulder, ignoring the fact that by doing so he was exposing himself to the fire from the trees, he fired twice. Sound bucketed through the room. Through narrowed eyes, Cal saw the running man, falter as one or both slugs took him in the back. He went down on one knee, hesitated there for a moment, his body clearly outlined in the silver moonlight. Then he somehow got to his feet and began to stumble towards the edge of the corral, covered by a vicious volley of fire from the rest of the outlaw band.

The agent grunted something through clenched teeth, then uttered a low sigh and slumped against the wall, the rifle falling from his fingers. Norma Holmes ran over to him, cradled his head in her arms. Cal stared off into the darkness, watching the flashing points of muzzle flame, loosing off a handful of shots at them before turning to look down at the wounded agent. The man's face was twisted with pain and there was an ominous black stain just visible on the front of his chequered shirt. It looked black, but it might just be that the wound was a ragged one, the bullet having entered across the man's chest, tearing through the flesh but not penetrating.

'I'll take care of him,' said the girl in a harsh whisper. 'Just you keep your eyes on those killers out there.'

Cal hesitated, then nodded to himself, let her do what she could for the other. It would take her mind off things, he thought, although even if they did manage to get out of this station alive, and had to take the wounded agent with them, there would be little they could do to alleviate his pain until they got him to a doctor.

The fire in the barn had now taken a firm hold. The straw there was as dry as tinder, and Cal recalled that there had been several large bales of it, piled almost to the roof. They had no chance of preventing the fire from spreading, even if they had been able to get out to it, and tackle it unhindered. The barn itself was only ten yards or so away at its nearest point and once that inferno reached its height, the flames could quite easily reach over to the station house itself. Already sparks were lifting high into the air, drifting in their direction as the wind caught them. He had a dreadful instant as he visualized what their own fate would be if they did not get out of the building quickly.

If only one of them could reach the corral and drag a few of the horses to the back of the building where no one seemed to be watching the place, they might stand a chance.

A sudden movement at the corner of his vision caused him to turn his head sharply. The two dark shadows moved quickly, running forward agilely. At first he thought they intended to move forward and drop into cover nearer the building. Then, too late, he saw that this was not their intention. One of them slipped the latch of the gate to the corral and a moment later, they had slipped inside, and were firing their sixguns into the air, driving the horses out into the open, stampeding them away from the station and out into the desert.

That was the end for them, he told himself savagely, as he fired at the two men, now moving back towards the trees. Without horses, they could never hope to leave this place. It would even be impossible for one of them to slip away unseen and ride for help to Red Rock.

'Yuh don't have a chance now,' called one of the men among the trees. His voice could just be heard above the savage crackling of the flames as they leapt ten, twenty feet into the air. Already, the heat of the fire could be felt in the room, burning on Cal's face as he stared out bleakly into the moonlight.

There was a sudden movement behind him and he swung sharply to see the two men running in from the other room. For a wild moment he thought that the outlaws had played it too smart for him and had rushed the rear of the building while the others had kept his attention concentrated on the front.

'They've driven off the horses from the corral,' shouted one of the men hoarsely. 'We can't fight them now. We've got to surrender. I'm prepared to go out there and give myself up. They can have all the money I've got with me.'

'Don't be a fool,' hissed Cal as the other moved forward, towards the door. 'You can't trust any of those critters. They'll shoot you in the back the minute you step outside.'

In reply, the other lifted the gun he held in his hand. The barrel was pointed straight at Cal's chest and he noticed that it was shaking slightly as the other stepped towards him, his face contorted.

'Just step to one side, mister, away from that door. I'll shoot you down if you try to stop me. I'm warning you. I mean to go out there and give myself up even if you do want to stay and fight it out with them afterwards. You don't stand a chance of getting away now. They've only got to squat out there and you're finished. Without mounts we can't hope to get away.'

Cal eyed him narrowly. There was little doubt that the other meant every word he said. He was scared, afraid for his own skin, clearly believing that all these outlaws wanted was their money and any valuable they carried with them.

'Even if you do get outside, they'll kill you,' he said swiftly. 'Now just trust me and you'll be all right.'

'Trust you!' The other almost screamed the words. 'Why should we trust you? You got us into this mess. You knew they had taken the desert trail and yet you brought us here when you could have continued all the way to Red

Rock, even if it had meant travelling through the night. Look at that man there.' He pointed a shaking finger at the wounded agent lying on the floor. There was a tremor in his voice as he went on: 'That's what will happen to all of us if we listen to this man.' As he spoke, he turned to face the others near the bar.

'Don't listen to him.' Norma Holmes spoke up sharply. 'Those men are cold-blooded killers. They won't leave a single one of us alive if we surrender to them. I own this stageline and I know what is at the back of this. They're takin' orders from men in Sherman City who want the line for themselves.'

The other advanced purposefully towards Cal, still holding the gun on him, his finger tight on the trigger. This was the worst kind of man to fight, thought Cal grimly. A man who believed he was in the right, a man who was scared yet held a gun and would use it to protect himself. He did not want to have to shoot the other down, even though he knew that he could lift his own gun and fire before the other had a chance to pull that trigger. The man was scared; and he couldn't really blame him. Besides, if he did that, even though it might be for the best, the others would never obey him.

Shrugging his shoulders, he moved to one side, but his gaze never once left the man's face.

'That's better. I'm glad that you can see sense,' muttered the other. He inched forward, edging towards the door. Reaching it, he twisted the handle, opened it a couple of inches and yelled loudly: 'I'm coming out with my hands lifted. I'm surrendering to you.'

For a moment, there was silence, then a mocking voice called. 'Just step on out then, mister, and toss your gun out before yuh.'

Obeying, the man hurled the Colt out into the dust. It landed with a dull thud and in that same moment, Cal moved. His left arm snaked out, caught the other around the neck, tightened like a noose, then heaved. Unable to help himself, the other was immediately thrown off balance by Cal's action. He uttered a single strangled cry, then fell back into the room as Cal slammed the door shut. Scarcely had he done so than a fusillade of shots rang out, the slugs tearing into the thick, tough wood of the door.

The man lay where he had fallen, staring up at Cal in the dimness, his face a pale blur, his throat muscles working as he strove to pull air down into his heaving lungs.

'Mebbe you'll believe me now,' grated Cal harshly. 'Those bullets were meant for you. If I hadn't moved, you'd have been standin' out there in the courtyard, in full view o' those critters and instead of hitting the door, those slugs would have perforated your hide.'

Gasping, the man scrambled to his feet, rubbed his neck with his fingers. 'You nearly strangled me there,' he muttered throatily.

'Better that than a belly full of lead,' retorted the other. He turned back to the window, knowing there would be no more fight from the other for the time being. The man had learned his lesson the hard way. Now, he would understand the fix they were in.

More slugs hummed across the room after cutting through the smashed windows. None of the outlaws seemed to want to come any closer. They seemed content to let them stay there until the heat from the blazing barn drove them out into the open. The second man, who had been standing near the bar, watching the proceedings closely came over. Anxiously, trying desperately to control the shaking in his voice, he asked: 'Is there any chance at all of getting out of here before those flames reach us and burn us alive?'

Cal pressed his lips into a hard, tight line. A riot of thoughts raced through his mind, half-confused. He levelled one of the Colts at a running shadow, but the slug missed and the man ducked back under cover once more.

'You see any of them varmints at the back of the house while you were watchin' there?' he demanded quickly.

'Why — no. Couldn't be certain but everything is as dark as night out there. They could be moving up from that direction.' He whirled as the thought struck him, then paused as Cal called:

'Hold it! You may be right. That's probably our only chance. This side of the building is lit up like day by that fire. But back yonder, it'll be like pitch and if we douse any lights and work our way out, we may get clear before they realize what's happened.'

'But without horses and with a wounded man on our hands. What sort of a chance do you call that?' Terror edged the man's voice and he backed away a little, watching Cal as though the other were mad.

Through clenched teeth, Cal said: 'You've got two other chances. Wait here until this place goes up like tinder around you, or step out into that courtyard yonder and get yourself filled with slugs. Which is it to be?'

A pause, then: 'Guess we got no other choice.' The man muttered something under his breath, then moved forward, stuffing the Colt into his waistband. He gave a helping hand to his companion, still kneeling on the floor. 'What about him?' He pointed to the agent. 'He's badly hurt and we can't get him to a doctor in time to do much for him anyway. He'll only hamper us, maybe shorten our chances of getting free.'

'Mebbe so,' Cal nodded. 'But we take him with us just the same. One of you can carry him when we get to the back door.'

'I'm damned if I will.'

'You'll be dead if you don't,' snapped Cal, and there was a deliberate, cold menace in his voice. He levelled the Colt in his right hand at the man's chest, saw the other flinch, then swallow quickly.

Cal turned to Norma. 'Just how bad

is he?' he asked tightly.

She glanced up at him. 'Not too badly hurt. He's still losing quite a lot of blood but I think I've managed to patch most of it.'

'Can we take him with us?'

She hesitated, then gave a quick nod. 'If it's either that or leave him here to be butchered by those devils, then we have no other choice.'

'I figured that.' He nodded to the two men. 'Take him by the arms and legs and carry him to the back.'

They obeyed him reluctantly. As they moved through the door, with the women following behind them, Norma turned to Cal. Her voice was only a husky whisper as she murmured, 'Tell me the truth, Cal. Even this way, our chances of escape are pretty slender, aren't they?'

He reached out, gripped her arm as he guided her to the door. 'Pretty slim,' he agreed. 'Even if we do manage to slip away from them without being seen, we still have fifteen or twenty miles of desert to cross and then the hills, before we reach either Red Rock or the railroad.'

She nodded and once more, he noticed the look of determination on her face, the curious lack of fear in her eyes. Then he moved around to the back of the bar, picked up the wooden barrel of water which had been placed there earlier, ready to be strapped to the rear of the stage, and slung it over his shoulders. At least, he could make as certain as possible that they did not die of thirst in the desert.

★　★　★

The others were waiting for him in the darkened room at the back of the station. They watched anxiously as he opened the door quietly and slipped out, standing with his back pressed tightly against the wall. Reaching the edge of the rickety porch there, he crouched down low, staring about him. It was an old scout's trick, getting his surroundings lined up against the sky to see better if anything moved. The moon was just edging over the tops of the tall trees in the near distance, flooding everything with a cold, eerie light and the tall cacti wore a shimmering sheen of powder-grey which made the whole world seem strange and unnatural. Head cocked to one side, he listened intently. There was still some shooting at the front of the building, but out here, everything was quiet and still. Nothing moved in the long shadows thrown by the moon as his eyes travelled from side to side, searching the empty wilderness that lay at the rear of the long corral, now empty and deserted. The outlaws had had plenty of time to work their way around the place if they had ever intended to do so. The very fact that there seemed to be no one there was disturbing in itself. He would have felt a trifle easier in his mind if he had caught a glimpse of someone watching the back of the building. It wasn't like these men to leave a place unguarded and unwatched at the back.

Perhaps they were relying on the fact that in this direction, there was nowhere they could run to. They would be out in the open, would be forced to keep on moving into the desert. The breeze was light and fitful as he moved to the wide end of the porch at the very side of the building and carefully inched his head around the corner. A pony neighed among the trees where the outlaws would have tethered their mounts. For one moment, the wild thought seeped into his mind that perhaps they might even have a chance of slipping into the trees from this direction, moving up on any men left behind to watch the horses and taking them by surprise. That way it would be possible for them to turn the tables on the outlaws with a vengeance, ride off with their mounts and leave them stranded, high and dry, at the way station, ready for the sheriff from Red

Rock to ride out with a posse and pick them up.

But he dismissed the thought almost as soon as it had entered his mind. The ground between them and the trees was too open. A man would be seen before he had taken half a dozen paces and shot down and that would give the game away for the rest of them. Turning, he motioned to the others to move out and across the open ground into the cacti and soapweed which grew in wild profusion on the edge of the space that had been cleared. The taller of the two men came out, staggering under the burden of the wounded agent, slung over his shoulder. He was the last to reach cover, then Cal followed, casting a quick glance over his shoulder as he ran. There was no sign from the trees that their escape had been noticed. But this did not ease the tension that had been climbing in his mind for the past hour. They were not out of trouble yet, not by a long way. He thought that the outlaws at the front of the house would lie low for a while, waiting for the blazing barn to do their dirty work for them, rather than risk more men trying to rush the place. He wondered if Kearney and the sheriff from Sherman City were there with those outlaws. It was possible. The sheriff had ridden out of town in a mighty hurry shortly before they had pulled out that morning and it seemed that the only place he could possibly have been heading for had been the outlaws' hideout, to warn them of the departure of the stage and to warn them to set a trap somewhere along the trail.

The others were crouched down in the chapparal in a loose bunch, breathing heavily from their exertions. The girl turned to him as he came up to them:

'Have they seen us?'

'I reckon not. If they had, there would have been some slugs sent after us. I figure we've probably got an hour, not longer, before they get nosy and start rushing the place. When they discover that we're gone, they'll ride after us. But they won't pick up our trail for some little time.'

'Not even back there?' muttered one of the men.

'Not a chance,' Cal shook his head. 'Don't know if you noticed it or not, but that ground was solid rock. Hardly any dust coverin' it either. Let's move out and put as much ground between them and ourselves as we can. We've got a few hours before dawn and after that it's goin' to be hot in the desert.'

'You know which way to go?' demanded the other harshly. 'I don't relish the idea of wanderin' around in circles in the desert yonder.'

'If you come with me, that's a risk you're goin' to have to take,' snapped Cal in a hushed tone. 'Now get movin' and quit talkin'.'

The journey through the rough ground that lay around the way station was a tremendous ordeal in the dark. The path they were forced to take, leading them between tall, upthrusting rocks, was narrow and winding, but the bright moon helped them in most places and in others, where the rocks hid the moonlight, they were forced to push their hands in front of them and feel their way forward. At their backs, the blazing barn still lit up the sky, giving them something by which to take their direction. So long as they kept that behind them, they were on the right trail, thought Cal fiercely. The hours passed slowly. Their progress was slow, too slow for Cal's liking, but he knew that it would be impossible to hurry them. They had to carry the wounded agent with them and the women were finding the going rough and difficult, their dresses were being torn and ripped by the clawing teeth of the rocks on either side of them and they stumbled and fell at regular intervals as their strength began to give out on them.

By dawn, Cal reckoned they had covered perhaps three miles. The terrain was still rough and rocky and in the pale, cold light of dawn, it looked terrible and forbidding. He shivered a little in the cold breeze that blew off the desert which lay in front of them, pulled the high collar of his jacket tighter around his neck.

'You reckon we can rest up for a while,' called one of the men hoarsely. His legs wavered under him as if they were made of rubber, unable to bear his weight any longer.

Cal looked about him, studying the terrain, then glanced quickly over his shoulder in the direction from which they had just come. There was, as yet, no sign of any pursuit, but he knew instinctively, with a sure certainty, that it would not be long in coming. Those men would not stay around the way station long once they found out what had happened. If their leader had any sense at all, he would split the bunch and send his men out in several different directions. That way, he could be sure of hunting them down eventually.

But the men and women were almost completely exhausted. He nodded slowly, pointed to a stretch of ground in the lee of one of the huge rocks. 'We'll rest there for a while,' he said harshly. 'But once the sun comes up, we'll have to move on. You understand that?'

'Sure, sure,' the men nodded, moved over to the rocky shelf beneath the wide overhang. The taller man laid down the agent, then straightened up with a grunt, rubbing his shoulders as he worked his limbs to restore some of the circulation. The women sank down in huddled heaps, leaning their heads back against the hard rock, eyes staring straight in front of them, their faces drawn and haggard with the terrible strain. Cal watched them closely for a moment, then shrugged and turned away. It was going to be a sight worse than this before they were through, he reflected wearily. If they considered they were going through hell now, it was as nothing compared with what they would be forced to suffer through the day. He could not afford to let them rest as long as he would have liked. He knew they were almost at the end of their endurance, yet he would have to force them to continue the trek within half an hour or so.

He lowered the water barrel from his shoulders and sank down beside them, his grim face tight. 'We'll rest until sun-up,' he said throatily. 'Then we'll have to move out. Those outlaws will be on our heels before long.'

'I don't think I'll ever feel warm again,' complained one of the women, pulling her shawl more tightly about her shoulders. 'I'll be glad when the sun does come up and there's a little warmth in the air.'

Cal smiled grimly. 'When the sun does rise, and we get out there in the desert,' he told her, 'you'll begin wishin' it was night time again.' His frown returned. 'This is nothing compared with the discomfort we've got to face during the day.'

Under the lee of the big rocky overhang, they got what rest they could while the dawn brightened in the east, the long streaks of grey stretching themselves across the heavens, then changing to scarlet and gold as the sun rose, bounding up from below the horizon, so that it seemed to virtually hurl itself headlong into the sky. Cal sat with his head back against the rock, staring down the slope they had just climbed. Lack of sleep and the long hard climb had told on him just as much as it had on the others. In spite of himself, his eyes kept lidding and closing, his head jerking forward on to his chest, the movement snapping him awake. Somehow, he must have dozed off, for the sound that woke him was one he had not heard when they had first moved into this patch of rock.

He was awake instantly, peering about him, every nerve stretched taut as he stared around the rocky ground trying to pick out what had woken him. Then he realized what it was and a little tremor of apprehension went through him. The ceaseless vibrant whine of the wind had risen in pitch until it shrieked softly in his ears and already, the dust and sand were being blown in little, scurrying clouds across the smooth rocks. With an effort, he dragged himself upright, stood for a moment with his hands on the rock to maintain his balance, then bent and shook the others awake.

The two men cursed feebly, but made no resistance. Getting to their feet, they looked about them in growing alarm. The heat had risen while they had been sleeping and now the sun shone through the scudding clouds of gritty sand, huge and red. Cal watched it grimly as the others stared about them. 'Walkin' ain't goin' to be easy for us if this breeze gets any worse,' he observed. He gave the others a wry smile. 'And it won't make keepin' to the trail easy, either.'

'Maybe we'd best wait here until it blows itself out,' suggested Norma.

Cal pointed back in the direction they had come during the night. 'It won't have wiped out our trail through the rocks,' he said tautly. 'They may have found it by now. If they catch us here we're finished.' His tone was quiet and deliberate.

Heaving the water barrel over his shoulders, he gestured to the others to pull out. The agent was still only semi-conscious. Most of the time he was quiet, did not seem to know what was happening.

Out in the open, the heat and the whiring clouds of sand struck them all forcibly. The wind was intermittent, not always blowing from the same direction, and this made things worse for them. It sent the hordes of tiny, gritty particles showering on to the clothing, into their eyes and noses, clogging their mouths and throats even though they lowered their heads against it and tried to breath slowly and easily. By the time they had progressed a further half mile, the wind had risen still more and instead of little sheets of sand and dust flying about them, the air was filled with millions of tiny, irritating grains which seemed to have the ability to probe anywhere. The sun shone through a deep red-orange fog which closed in about them, shutting them off completely from the rest of the world. Cal moved in the lead, seeking the trail which was becoming steadily more and more obliterated in front of them. The drifting sand filled all of the hollows among the rocks, surging over the trail, swirling around his ankles. In places, the tall basaltic formations which bordered the trail at this point, loomed like great ghostly fingers out of the gloom. They piled up in a strange nightmare confusion, so that it was impossible to use any of them as landmarks, in that terrible dimness where everything looked alike and it was difficult to distinguish one rock formation from another.

They moved slowly now, tensed and cautious. The wind keened in their ears and the dusty rattle of the sand against the rocks completely blotted out any sound of pursuit there might have been at their backs. Speaking little, they made their way forward through the sweeping storm, unable to see more than half a dozen feet in any direction, blinded by the searing grains of sand which the wind hurled at their faces.

By the time they had moved out of the rocks into the flatness of the desert, the storm was even worse than before. In this stretching wilderness there was no cover, nothing to break the force of the wind and from the throbbing whine, the sound of it rose to a high-pitched wail that shrieked at the ears until they hurt with the roar of it. Eyes screwed up, the edges of his jacket whipping about him, Cal strode forward, pausing every few moments to look back and check that they were all there. It would be so damnably easy for one or more of them to get lost in a storm such as this, which was something he had never bargained for when he had suggested that they should try to make a run for it.

One thing was certain however, it would hamper any men who were riding after them. This storm would spook the horses like little else on earth, almost as much as a rattler, and the riders would have a difficult time controlling them. Indeed, it was unlikely that they would make as much progress as they were on foot. For long minutes, it was a case of moving forward, with heads ducked down low on their chests, trying to shield themselves from the full fury of the driving storm with their arms. Whistling and screaming, the wind roared about them, sometimes ceasing and then abruptly buffeting them from another, totally unexpected, direction, so that there was little chance of retaining one's balance. In the blinding, diffuse haze that needled them mercilessly, their progress was slowed to inches each dragging minute, and it was soon obvious that they could not go on much longer like this, that they would have to find someplace where they could find shelter until it had blown over.

'It's time to quit,' he yelled to the leading man. He did not know whether the other had picked out his words, but the man nodded to show that he had understood the gist of what he had said. 'We'll have to find shelter until it blows itself out. May not last too long.'

The wind and the scouring particles of sand whipped the words from his lips and flung them mockingly into the whirling maelstrom of sound that roared about them. It was more than ten minutes later, when Cal spotted the tall ridge that loomed up on their left and moved towards it. For several yards, it was compounded of completely smooth rock, obviously scoured and polished by centuries of such storms. Then he came across the deep cleft in it, a cleft that went back into the rock for more than ten feet. Signalling the others, he guided them into it, then pushed in himself. Here, there was room for them to squat on the smooth ground and space to breathe, the wind soughing past the opening and losing itself out on the hard face of the desert. Nobody spoke as they squatted there, listening to the terrible keening of the wind and the still more frightening rush of sand and dust along the rock wall.

★   ★   ★

Savagely, Scott Kearney strode into the room at the rear of the way station, stood for a moment, staring about him. Then he spun on the two men at his back.

'Why were there no men watchin' the back of the building?' he snarled viciously.

'They was all in the front of the station,' growled a tall, black-bearded man. He jerked a thumb in the direction of the front room where the flames, started by sparks from the barn and fanned by the wind, already had a firm hold. The roof too, had caught fire and was blazing furiously.

Kearney paused, his face a mask of bitter fury as he swung to let his glance sweep over the others until it lit on the tall figure of the man who still wore the silver star on his shirt.

The sheriff let his own gaze slide away from the furious look on Kearney's tight features. 'There ain't nuthin' out yonder but desert,' he mumbled, obviously trying to defend himself and the others. 'We never reckoned they'd be fool enough to try to git away in that direction. Not with the passengers they had with 'em. Three women won't stand a chance out there.' He moved across to the door, looked out into the greying light of the early dawn. 'There's a storm blowin' up out there too. They won't git far. If we ride out now, we ought to catch up on 'em before they've gone more'n a few miles.'

'You dogblasted fool,' grated Kearney savagely. 'Even if they slipped out from under your very noses and went that way, it don't mean to say they'll keep on travellin' in that direction. They could be anywhere within fifty square miles of rough country by now, possibly holed up in the rocks until the storm blows itself out. How d'you propose that we find 'em before they get too far?'

The sheriff shrugged, glanced about him at the others. 'Reckon the only thing we can do, is split up and ride out in different directions. That way, we ought to spot 'em before long. The desert is mighty flat once they get out there and if we ride the ridges, we can see for miles when this storm blows over.'

Kearney grimaced, then shrugged. In the circumstances, it was the only thing they could do. He swallowed his anger with an effort, then nodded. 'All right, if you want it that way, we'd better ride.' At the doorway, he paused, looked back as the others came crowding after him.

'One thing might help us,' he said thinly. 'We've got to credit that jasper,

Mannix, with a modicum of sense. He knows that on foot they won't be able to make fast time and they'll only have a certain amount of water with 'em, to divide among seven. He'll have to head straight for Red Rock or back to Sherman City. Reckon it's about the same distance both ways, so it's a toss up which way he goes. There's that stream in the hills above Snake Pass. But in the other direction, there's no waterhole between here and Red Rock. Still, he might try that way to throw us off the scent. We'll split into two. Sheriff, you head back to Snake Pass. I'll take the other bunch and we'll head out for Red Rock.'

The lawman nodded. 'An' if we do find 'em,' he muttered, 'what do we do with 'em?'

Kearney smiled thinly. 'You ought to know better than to ask me that,' he said harshly. 'They all know too much about me and my interest in this matter. But as far as Mannix is concerned, be sure that he dies slow.'

'Sure thing.' The sheriff grinned unpleasantly. His eyes gleamed a little as if he were suddenly aware that he had some power and leadership now. Then he whirled on the bunch next to him. 'Mount up, men, you heard what Mister Kearney said. We're to hunt down this bunch and finish 'em.'

After the others had ridden out, Scott Kearney called together the men who were to ride with him, made them tie their bandannas over their mouths and nostrils. Already the wind had become whipped up and little eddies of dust were whirling and scudding across the courtyard, twisting in tiny spirals among the trees and over the now-empty corral. He swung up into the saddle, feeling a sense of lust and triumph in him. When Scott Kearney wanted anything done, he thought inwardly, one got real action. The feeling made him eager to be on his way, to show these outlaws just what kind of a helling wolf he was.

They rode out in single file into the

rocks that lifted half a mile from the rear of the way station. By now, the whole structure was on fire, the roof burning fiercely. They had gone less than a quarter of a mile when a rending crash made Kearney turn abruptly in the saddle. Glancing back, he saw that the roof had fallen in and that there was now only a burning shell left of what had once been the way station. A grin passed over his coldly handsome features. When the stageline became his, he would see to it that a bigger and better station was built here. For a moment, he watched the place burn, flames leaping high into the greying heavens. Then he deliberately turned his back on the scene of destruction and urged his mount forward along the twisting, rocky trail.

The wind continued to lift once the sun came up, blurring details and making it difficult to see where they were. In front of him, the trail wound in and out of the rocks and there were no signs of the party they were trailing.

The eagerness was still in him, a force that drove him on, but although he raked spurs over the mount's flanks, the animal refused to go any faster, seemed to know that there was danger and discomfort ahead for them and wanted little of it. Cursing a little under his breath, he confronted himself with the knowledge that progress would certainly be slower for the others travelling on foot.

When they reached the badlands, the sun was already high above the horizon, glaring redly and ominously through the swirling dust haze. His horse was soaked in sweat and lather, but he continued to push it cruelly. It rolled in its stride, and its breathing was a sobbing heave which he could hear clearly even over the keening whistle of the wind. Clattering in and out of the stony gulches and arroyos, scattering the rocks and pebbles underfoot, sending them bouncing and rolling down the slope, they clattered among the rocks, heedless of ambush.

One of the men gigged his mount and drew level with him, his head bent sideways as he called loudly, his voice strangely muffled through the bandanna. 'Are yuh sure that we're on the right trail?'

Kearney screwed up his eyes as he lifted his head momentarily. Through thinned lips he snarled: 'How do I know? It's impossible to see ten yards in this storm. We'll just have to keep ridin' until we either spot 'em, or know that we're ahead of 'em. Which ever way it is, we'll have 'em cut off once they try to make for the desert.'

It was the best they could do. For all he knew, Mannix and the others could be holed up in any of the rocky clefts that littered this part of the territory. There were a hundred places the party could hide and he and his men could ride within ten feet of them without knowing they were there. And if Mannix did hear the sound of the horses, it was highly unlikely he would open fire on him for fear of giving away his position. No, he'd be too crafty a man for that. He'd make those with him keep quiet until he and his men had ridden past.

He lifted his head again, in spite of the full fury of the blinding grains of dust that lashed at his exposed flesh, and peered bleakly ahead. He knew that they were pushing their horses to the limit, that if they kept on this way, without resting up and giving the animals a chance to blow and get their strength back, they might kill them all and in this country that could be fatal. At best, it would place them all on a level with Mannix and the others.

A deep breath filled his chest, the hot air going down like fire into his lungs. Finally, he made his decision, swung round and pointed towards the rising shape of the buttes, urging his mount into the shelter of the rock. The others followed swiftly, climbing down and crouching behind their mounts.

6

State of Seige

The storm died down late in the morning. Slowly, the last breath of wind subsided and a great stillness lay over everything. Where the trail had once been, there was only a river of sand, ankle-deep, which had obliterated it completely. Cal sat with his back against the wall of the rocky cleft and stared at the others out of red-rimmed eyes. His face felt sore and tender where the grains of sand and dust had abraded the flesh.

'I reckon it's over for the time bein',' he croaked. His throat felt scoured and parched and he poured a little water into the tin mug and handed it to each of the others before taking a swig himself. His dried-up mouth soaked up the liquid almost at once so that there seemed to be little left to cleanse his throat. But although he could have drunk ten times that amount, and he knew how the others must be feeling, he deliberately corked the barrel, pushing the bung in tightly, then heaved himself to his feet with an effort, and stepped to the opening of the cleft. Through cracked lips, he muttered: 'Reckon we might as well get along while the light lasts. No tellin' when those critters will be on our trail.'

The other men stirred and got to their feet shakily, came over and stared about them. The last puffs of dust had just begun to settle and already the sky was clearing almost miraculously. Blue appeared through the golden red haze which had covered the area only a few minutes before. The light of the sun, at its zenith now, increased swiftly in brilliance, until it was an eye-searing white, impossible to look at.

'Do we still have to drag him along?' demanded one of the men harshly. He nodded down at the agent, lying inert on the rocky ledge. 'We only have so much water left and I don't see any point in wasting it on a dying man, a man who'll only slow us up anyway.'

'Maybe so, but he still comes with us. That wound in the shoulder ain't so bad if we can only get him to a doctor.'

'And what chance is there of that?' muttered the other man. His clothing was torn and streaked with dust and neither of them looked much like city gentlemen now. 'You said yourself that we had more than fifteen miles of desert to cross, and with the women, it's going to be a slow job.'

Cal eyed the other with a careful frown, under his brows. Certainly the journey had been a big strain on them all, even during the few hours they had been travelling, but that was no excuse for leaving a wounded man to die when there was still a chance to save him. He clamped his teeth tightly together, motioned to the agent. 'We'll take turns at carryin' him,' he said thinly. 'That way we'll share the burden.'

Grumbling, one of the men lifted the agent and slung him over his shoulders. When they were ready, Cal gave the area another quick glance, then motioned them forward at a slow pace. The women had regained a little of their strength during the rest from the storm, but he doubted if they would be able to travel too far without wanting another rest. Besides, he thought inwardly, those dresses were not exactly the right kind of wear to trek through the desert. Modesty or not, they would soon have to tuck them up about their knees.

Ahead of them, a shallow ravine dipped down to the desert proper. The floor of the ravine was of bare rock, showing no tracks of any kind. Way ahead, the defile opened out into a wider space beneath a tall bluff below which were two huge rocks which thrust themselves up out of the flat terrain, almost like twin sentinels marking the gateway into the desert. They passed through these without once looking up. From a stage coach, such things might have aroused some interest, but trekking like this, on foot, with the blistering heat of the desert all about them, it was difficult to become interested in anything but finding water and shade and a place of rest.

Slowing his pace, he dropped back a little until he came alongside Norma Holmes. The girl glanced up and gave him a brave smile, but it could not hide the lines of strain that showed on her face. 'Reckon you can handle the two ladies, Norma?' he asked thickly.

She gave him a slow nod. 'I think so, Cal. But from here, it all looks so hopeless. Pretty soon, they're going to start thinking that may be they might have had a better chance giving themselves up.'

'Those *hombres* would have killed 'em all for sure. Make no mistake about that, Norma.'

'I know. I've lived in this country all my life and I know how these men act, but these other people here haven't run up against men like that. They simply don't understand that anyone could hold life so cheap that they would deliberately shoot down an unarmed man as soon as look at him.'

She stopped then and a tiny shiver ran through her body. Cal knew that she was thinking of Kearney and the sheriff, knew that none of them could expect any pity from men such as that.

The hours passed, long tormented things. The heat had increased until they seemed to be moving through a burning sea of air that gave them no respite. Every breath they took burned in their lungs and although the dust storm had subsided, the glare from the desert made it difficult to see for any distance. Regularly, Cal paused to stare behind him, watching for the first sign of trouble, knowing that it would not be long before those riders caught up with them. When that happened, their only chance would be to find some defensive position, get the women inside and shoot it out with the outlaws.

The sun was finally going down when they dragged themselves wearily on to a low shelf of ground, the only stretch that lifted above the flatness of the desert. Dejection settled heavily on Cal as he stood there, shading his eyes against the sun, gazing out over the savage wilderness that lay ahead of them, facing the inescapable fact that they were still only at the beginning of their journey, their misery and danger. In that ghastly desert, their chances of survival for long, were low. In that wild and barren country, a man could lose himself quite easily and years later, another party crossing it, would stumble on a pile of sun-bleached bones, all that remained of him. This land wanted nothing of man, rejected him with everything at its disposal. The dunes were swarming with rattlers and other species of equally poisonous snakes and in the old days, even the Indians had kept clear of the place, skirting it well to the north as testified by their trails in that area.

Behind them, the vast stretch of desert which they had crossed was void and silent, showing no sign of movement right to the shimmering horizons, no indication of the presence of any living thing.

'We'll make camp here for the night,' he said quietly. 'We'll set watch at intervals during the night, and I'd like the man on watch to remember that if he does drop off to sleep when he's supposed to be keeping look out, he'll be the first man to die if they attack us without warnin'.'

★ ★ ★

The ledge was long, perhaps half a mile in length, and lifted some thirty feet above the rest of the desert. In the bright moonlight, Cal sat on a small mound and stared intently about him, eyes taking in everything, his face tense and inscrutable. The sand would muffle the sound of horses, even in the quiet that had dropped about them with the setting of the sun. The moon had risen shortly after dark, giving plenty of light to see by, but throwing shadows over the dunes and gullies. A man's imagination could run riot with him out here, he reflected.

He rolled himself a smoke, ducked low as he lit it, keeping himself in the shadow of the mound, deliberately easing his body into lower ground. Even the faint red glow from the tip of the cigarette could be spotted half a mile away by a keen-eyed marksman. He smoked slowly, feeling some of the warmth come back into his body.

It was almost midnight when he first picked out the sound of riders in the distance. The faint drumming of hoofs could just be heard and it was impossible to estimate how far away they were, nor how many there were in the bunch. But of one thing he was sure. They could be none other than the outlaws, hunting them down in the moonlight. The desert that ran away from the bottom of the ledge was flat and wide and he moved swiftly forward to the far edge of it, peering out intently into the night. If any of the others woke and heard the sound, he hoped they would remain still and silent. The slightest movement now might be enough to give them away.

At first, he could see nothing in the pale silver moonlight, as he searched with eyes and ears, every nerve and fibre in his body taut with apprehension. Then he saw the bunch of riders, clustered close together. He reckoned they were the best part of a mile distant, but edging in their direction. If they continued on their course, they would pass within a couple of hundred yards of the ledge where they had made camp. Moving slowly and surely, he wriggled back to the others, woke the girl first, motioning her to silence as she struggled to get up. It was impossible to make out the expression on her shadowed face, but there was tension visible in every curve of her body as she held herself taut and rigid.

'What is it?' she whispered in a tight, little voice.

'Those critters who've been tailin' us all day,' he murmured softly. 'Lie still and whatever happens, don't make a sound if you value your life. They may pass us by if we keep still. I'll wake the others, just in case we have to make a fight for it.'

One by one, he woke the men and women, clapping his hand over their mouths as they struggled awake. Less than two minutes since he had spotted the horsemen in the distance, they were all awake with the exception of the wounded agent, lying flat in the small hollow, pressing their bodies as close as possible into the sand, their hearts thudding rapidly in their chests, holding their breath until it hurt in their lungs. The riders came closer, the muffled sound of hoofbeats moving ahead of them. Cal reckoned there were possibly twelve or fifteen of them, and that told him instantly that Kearney, if he had been leading them back at the way station, had done as he had figured he would, and split the bunch, sending one group out towards Snake Pass and Sherman City, determined not to miss a trick.

A low, muttering moan came from somewhere at Cal's back and he turned his head with a muttered curse. The agent had woken up and was murmuring deliriously in his comatose condition. He had to be stopped before he gave away their hiding place. Swiftly, he edged back to the semi-conscious man, clapped his hand over the other's mouth, holding it tightly in place, even though the other tried to struggle feebly against the hold.

Had those outlaws heard the faint sound? They would be listening for anything that might give them a clue to the whereabouts of the folk they were hunting. But they rode straight on, not deviating from their path. Narrowing his eyes against the glare of the moonlight, he thought he recognized the man in the lead, pushing his mount on at a cruel, punishing pace. There was certainly something vaguely familiar about him, and he felt certain it was Scott Kearney who led that bunch of killers. He wondered if the girl had seen him too, wondered what thoughts must have been passing through her mind at that moment if she had. It must have come as a tremendous shock to her to realize that the man she had almost promised to marry would lead these men in an attempt to kill her, to hunt her down like an animal.

But it was no use worrying about that now. He felt a little shiver pass through him as the cold night air struck through his clothing. Briefly, he caught the murmur of voices as the men rode by. Once, he heard a hoarse, bellowing laugh. Then the bunch had ridden by and the sound of hoofbeats faded into the night and the moonlight. He let his breath out of his lungs in slow pinches, then removed his hand from the agent's mouth and pushed himself up on to his feet. It still seemed scarcely credible that the others had ridden by, as close as that, and had not seen them.

'They've gone,' he said softly. 'But we ain't safe yet, by a long way. They'll ride on for a little while and then start to backtrack.' He did not mention the fact that now the outlaws were between them and safety. There was enough for the others to worry about at the moment without telling them that.

There would be no more sleep for any of them that night and he knew that although this was perhaps the best defensive position they would ever find in the whole of the desert this side of Red Rock, their best chance was to start moving again, away from the trail those outlaws had taken. If Kearney did realize that he and his men must have passed them somewhere along the trail, the chances were that they would backtrack close to their original trail.

'Sorry to force you to move after havin' had so little sleep,' Cal said, addressing the three women, 'but I figure that it won't be long before those men head back this way. They probably spotted the ledge as they rode past but didn't figure it worth their while to stop and check. When they return, they won't make that mistake a second time and we don't have much chance of fighting them all off, even here.'

The taller of the two men, surprisingly, nodded his head in agreement. 'I understand,' he said harshly. 'I don't know what we can do, but I reckon it should be easier walking in the moonlight when the heat's off.'

'This is a bad business,' acknowledged Cal. 'We're in a spot. I reckon that bunch tallied up to fifteen or so men, more than we can handle with any sort of a chance. My own guess is that they'll go on for maybe another five miles before headin' back. By that time, we could be a mile to the south of here, well away from their trail.'

They moved out, stumbling a little in the dimness, reached the end of the ridge of ground and moved down into the shifting sand of the desert. It was a relatively simple matter to take their directions from the moon and stars and in the cool, clear night air, they made good progress. Fear drove most of them on, Cal realized. Now that they had caught their first sight of the men who were trailing them, they all realized just how close death might be to them. It was this, more than anything else, which gave them the necessary strength and endurance to keep on moving, even when their arms and legs were numb with the intense cold and movement had become a mechanical rhythm that seemed to go on and on with no end.

By dawn, he considered that they were safe for a little while. Everyone was in a bad way now. Carrying the injured agent had called for all the strength they had, even though they had taken it in turn. In the end, one man could carry the inert weight for only a little way before dropping to his knees, his strength utterly spent. Then too, there had been the water barrel to carry with them. Without it they would certainly die of thirst within a few hours, once the sun rose bringing the dry, lip-cracking heat with it. They rested up in a small clump of mesquite and soapweed, almost the only plants which were able to grow in this terrible wilderness.

The heat, when it came was almost a welcome relief from the terrible cold of the night just past, but within an hour, it had soaked down into their bodies until they were sickened by the glare, the sweat boiling from them, eyes and flesh burned by the vicious inferno air that pressed down on them like the flat of a mighty hand, crushing them utterly. Every breath brought the rawness into their throats and lungs, and Cal watched them all eyeing the water barrel covertly and knew what was in their minds.

It was the shorter of the two men who first voiced the thoughts of them all. Hoarsely, he muttered: 'You going to keep that water until we get to Red Rock, Mannix? Can't you see that the women are dying of thirst? Surely a few mouthfuls isn't going to make all that much difference to our chances of survival.'

'Seems to me that you don't know the first thing about this territory, mister,' Cal replied. 'We've still got another two days' march ahead of us before we get within sight of Red Rock. Since we left that ridge during the night we've been trackin' a detour south of the stage trail. Unfortunately, that's added quite a few miles to our trail.'

The other drew his lips over his teeth. His hands clenched themselves into tightly-knotted fists as he glared at Cal. 'You was the one who suggested that we stood a good chance coming with you. How do you know that those men would have shot us down if we'd given ourselves up like they said? They didn't want anything from us but money and gold. That's all they ever want.'

'You seem to have a mighty high opinion of outlaws,' Cal retorted harshly. 'You saw for yourself what happened when your friend tried to toss out his gun and go out of there with his hands lifted. They fired a volley of shots at the door. If I'd let him take one step outside that station, he would have got half a dozen slugs in him. That's the kind of critters they are, and don't you ever forget it.'

The other relapsed into a sullen silence. Whether or not he believed him, Cal did not care at the moment. Perhaps he and the girl were the only ones in the party who knew just how short their chances of getting across the desert alive were. It was essential that they should conserve every drop of water that they had, ration it carefully, as they had in the cavalry during the war so many weary years before. His training then had come in handy now. It had enabled him to be fairly certain that they were not wandering around in circles as so many people might when there were no landmarks.

It was useless to try to get the others

to continue the journey while the sun was still high. There was little shade here and all the time they had to keep a sharp lookout for the rattlers who came into the bushes out of the direct glare of the sun. A bite from one of them and they would lose a member of the party.

★ ★ ★

For several hours, they were forced to endure a purgatory on earth, the undiluted hell of heat and light which left them weak and sick. The women were so weak now, that Cal doubted their ability to move when the night came, but he knew that he had to force them to continue, that it would be death to stay here for another twelve hours. There had been scarcely a breath of wind all day, and their tracks since they had left the ridge would be clearly visible in the sand, leading Kearney and his men after them as clearly as if they had signposted the way.

In the late evening, when the sky

blazed with scarlet and hot pink over the mountains to the east, they moved out from the bushes, struggling to their feet, tongues moving over cracked lips. He allowed them each an extra sip of the warm water, then corked the barrel and hefted it over his shoulders, staggering now under the weight. He guessed it was half empty now and things were going to be tight before they reached the end of the trail.

He gave the others a sidelong glance as they staggered forward, both men now carrying the wounded agent between them. During the day, the other's condition had worsened considerably. The sand had worked its way into the bandages covering the wound during the storm in spite of everything they had been able to do to prevent it and the edges of the wound had turned a dark purple. There could be an infection there now, Cal thought inwardly, and that made it more imperative than ever that they should get him to a doctor as soon as possible if he was to have a chance of staying alive. Occasionally, throughout the day, he had regained consciousness and at times, he seemed to know what was happening, but most of the time, he rambled on under his breath, muttering curses and phrases which had no meaning to his bearers.

Norma Holmes was still bearing up well under the strain, but he saw the shadows which had come to her eyes and the tightness in her face. She would keep going until she dropped, he knew that. But there had to be an end to their strength and endurance sometime, and it was only a question of when it would come. Every hour, he had expected trouble from the outlaws. They would still be on their trail, that was for sure. Nothing would shake them off, not so long as Scott Kearney rode with them. This was the showdown which both men knew had to come and neither of them would try to wriggle out of it. But Cal wished that the odds had been a little more even than they were.

The reds and golds faded abruptly and they moved on into a deep blue world of dark shadows, the heat of the day dissipating rapidly now that the sun had gone down. With a clear, cloudless sky above them, it radiated swiftly into the still air, the desert cooling down swiftly too. As he walked after the others, Cal felt the worry nag at him incessantly, rubbing his nerves raw with the tense uneasiness. Why had Kearney not caught up with them during the day when they had been forced to stop and rest? On horseback, it would have taken him only a couple of hours to cover that distance from the ridge and he had men with him who could read trails as well as the Indians. It was unlikely that they had missed them completely; and it was all of Texas to five cents that Kearney would finish off what he was trying to do. Cal could not decide exactly how he would do it, but it would certainly bode ill for all of them. Perhaps Kearney was playing cat and mouse with them; had spotted them earlier in the day and had stood off, shadowing them across the desert, knowing that he would be able to strike at any time, feeling completely sure of himself.

The feeling of utter helplessness rose within him, blotting out everything else. It stayed with him for the next few hours as they stumbled forward in the pitch darkness, with only the stars and eventually the moon to guide them.

At length, they reached a stretch of rough country that lifted clear of the desert, an area of tumbled boulders and tall, spiring rocks, etched into strange and fantastic shapes by long ages of sun and rain. Behind a massive spire of rock lay a maze of crags and immense bosses of stone, piled high in titanic confusion. They paused on the rim of this vast basin, uncertain. There would be no water up here, but it might take all night to work their way around it, taking them miles from their original trail. If they were forced to deviate too far from it, there was a very definite chance that they might lose their way altogether, miss Red Rock and wander to their deaths in the desert that lay beyond the township.

'Well,' grunted one of the men, pausing to eye Cal tightly, 'do we go on through that, or try to cut around it?'

'We go through,' said Cal instantly. 'We can't afford to try to find a way around. It would take far too long and another thing. If those outlaws do catch up with us sometime during the night, this place is as good as any to stand them off. In here, four or five men could hold off an army.'

'For how long?' pointed out the other. 'We only have a limited amount of ammunition and water.'

'You've a point there,' Cal agreed, 'but it makes no difference.' He led the way up through the twisting maze of rocks. There was a narrow trail of sorts, possibly cut by prospectors in the years gone by, seeking gold in the hills. This was the sort of place they would have flocked to in the pioneering days before the war. Now the hills would be empty, deserted.

They were well into the rocks when they picked out the faint tattoo of sound in the distance. At first, it was only a starved echo, but it came nearer, resolved itself into hoofbeats, a large bunch, undoubtedly that which they had spotted the previous night. Icy nerve-thrills kept running up and down Cal's backbone as he paused and stared back into the moonlight, trying to pick out the riders against the darker background of the horizon. The desert below them gleamed a pale silver and it was not difficult to pick out the cloud of dust which marked the position of the riders.

'They're headin' this way,' he called sharply. 'Quickly! Into the rocks.'

'Maybe they'll pass us by as they did before,' muttered one of the men.

'Not a chance.' Cal shook his head as he helped Norma into the rocks. 'They must have been trailin' us all day. They know exactly where we are this minute.'

'How long before they reach us?' asked Norma breathlessly.

Cal cast another glance towards the oncoming men. 'Ten, maybe fifteen, minutes at the most.'

'What do we do now?' asked the tall man sharply. 'Why aren't we going on further into the rocks?'

Cal shook his head. His voice was thoughtful as he replied: 'Wouldn't do us any good. This is as good a place as any to make a stand. At least we can see 'em all the way up the trail and there ain't no other way up that I can make out.'

'Even so we don't have a chance of holding off that bunch of gunmen.'

Cal laid his glance on the other. 'If you can handle a gun, mister, this is the best chance you're goin' to get. Now snap out of sight behind those rocks and don't open up on these men until I give the signal. That goes for both of you, otherwise you'll spook 'em all into cover and we'll — '

He broke off at a sudden shout from the other man. Whirling, he saw that he had laid the stage agent down on the rocks and had clambered up a sharp incline, and was now standing on a small ledge, pointing at something out of sight, over the tops of the rocks.

Quickly, Cal scrambled up beside him. 'Down there in the hollow,' said the other excitedly. 'There's a hut of some sort. Wouldn't it be better to hole up there?'

'Could be,' Cal admitted hesitantly. The hut was some distance from the rocks which circled it and to get to it, the outlaws would have to cross that open space and they could bring fire to bear on them. 'Get down and bring the others. We can certainly take a look-see. Might be the very place for us.'

While the other moved back down the slope, Cal went forward warily. It was most likely that the cabin had been abandoned several years before by one of the prospectors, but it was as well to take no unnecessary chances. There were no lights showing and the door hung on twisted, rusty hinges. Kicking it open, one of the Colts ready in his hand, he went inside, peered about him in the pitch blackness. Moving forward, he struck something hard with his knee, reached out and ran his fingers over the table in the middle of the room. Carefully, he edged his way around it. By now, his eyes were becoming adjusted to the gloom and he was able to make out objects faintly. There was something dark against the rear wall of the cabin and he made his way forward. His fingers encountered a shovel and a couple of sieve pans propped carefully against the wall. At some time in the past, he figured, the owner of this place had simply placed everything in position and walked out, never to return.

The others came into the cabin just as he located the small barrels piled high against the corner. There was something familiar about them, but he was unable to say what it was. One of the men came over, stood beside him, trying to see.

'You got something there?' he asked softly.

'I'm not sure. Strike a match and I'll check. But be careful. There's just a chance we may be in luck and I wouldn't want an accident to happen here.'

'Accident?' There was a faint tremor of anxiety in the man's voice as he struck a sulphur match. By the red flare, Cal leaned forward and inspected the barrels, then let a long sigh drift out from his lungs. He stared up at the other in the dying flare of the match.

'Like I figured,' he said quietly, but there was a new note in his voice now. 'We're in luck. If we work fast, this may help us to even terms with those *hombres* a little.'

'Why, what is it, Cal?' Norma's voice reached him from the dimness near the middle of the room.

'Barrels of gunpowder,' he replied, with a note of triumph in his tone. He turned to the man beside him. 'Check and see if you can find any fuse. There's sure to be some around.'

Carefully he dragged a couple of the heavy barrels out of the corner, hefting them under each arm. He moved purposefully towards the open doorway.

'What do you intend to do?' Norma came forward and stood beside him.

Cal smiled mirthlessly. 'This time it's our turn to lay a trap for those killers,' he muttered harshly. 'Over here,' he called to the man in the corner of the room as the other remarked that he had found the fuse. 'I'll need you to help me place the powder.'

* * *

Leaning forward in the saddle, Scott Kearney pointed towards the low hills which shone eerily in the moonlight directly ahead of them. They had ridden hard during the past hour from where they had rested up most of the day. It had been easy following the party on foot after they had located their sign on the low ridge some miles back to the north. Evidently they were not taking time to try to wipe out their trail and he guessed that was either carelessness on Mannix's part, or they were too far gone to worry. It was possibly the latter, he reckoned.

He knew now that they were carrying a wounded man with them, and the three women were certain to slow them up. Inwardly, he had hoped to catch up with them before they had reached those rocks. It would have been a far simpler matter to have finished them out there on the desert. Now he would have to go get them out of the rocks and that would be a far from easy matter. It would also mean gunplay, with the possible loss of some of his men if the others decided to fight. At the moment, he wasn't sure whether they would or not. Certainly the men Mannix had with him would have no stomach for a fight with professional gunmen like those he had at his back and this was no quarrel of theirs. He speculated on the possibility of getting them to turn against Mannix. That way, he could be sure of winning the gunfight, without too much danger to himself or the men who rode with him. Not that he really cared much about these outlaws. They were useful only so long as he needed them. When they had finished the job, they were finished too as far as he was concerned.

He reined his mount as they came up to the wall of rock which faced them, rising sheer out of the flatness of the desert. Quickly, he scanned the dark jumble of boulders for any sign of Mannix and his party, but could see nothing. This was new country to him, well off the beaten trail into Red Rock, and he knew he would have to go warily if he wasn't to fall into a trap. They might try to bushwhack his bunch, knowing that they were being pursued and would be sure to watch their back trail.

Wheeling his mount, he faced the

bunch of men behind him. 'Any of yuh men know these hills?' he rasped harshly.

'I do,' muttered one of the men, urging his mount forward a little. 'Come prospectin' here once, several years ago. They reckon there's gold here, but I never found any.'

'Where d'you reckon Mannix and his party would hide if they meant to ambush us along the trail?'

The man scratched his chin thoughtfully for a moment. 'Reckon the best place would be up yonder.' He pointed to where a large overhang shadowed the trail. 'If I recollect rightly, there's an old abandoned mine workin' there, derelict now, but the cabins are probably still in pretty good shape. They could hole up in one of them, shoot it out with us.'

It made sense. Kearney nodded tersely. He sat tall in the saddle for a long moment, hands resting on the saddle horn, speculating. It was dark in those rocks and unless they went cautiously, they could ride straight into a trap. If Mannix had somehow talked the other men into helping him, probably warning them what their fate was likely to be if they fell into his hands, the three of them could hold off his bunch for quite a while, at least until their stock of ammunition ran out. And he and his men would have to expose themselves to their fire.

He pressed his lips tightly together into a thin, hard line. The trail up into the rocks was hard to see in the pale moonlight, but he motioned the men forward in single file, moving into the labyrinth of rocks. It was an eerie feeling, one he did not like at all, knowing that at any moment a gun might blast from behind one of the rocks, splitting the night silence into screaming fragments, the leaden impact of the slug knocking him out of his saddle. Little thrills of ice kept creeping up and down his spine and he tried not to keep glancing back over his shoulder as he rode, knowing that any show of fear or weakness on his part would inevitably reflect on the men with him. Wild at the best of times, they might ride out on him if they once considered that he was too afraid to go on.

There was a Remington carbine thrust into the scabbard just by the side of the saddle, but he kept it there, knowing that if danger did present itself, it would come quick and sudden, without warning, and a sixgun would be the best weapon to deal with it. He plucked one of the heavy Colts from its holster at his waist and held it tightly in his hand, finger bar-straight across the trigger as he rode.

The pale moonlight glimmered weirdly on the tips of the tall pinnacles of rock which lifted sheer on either side of the winding trail. Several times his mount halted of its own accord, as its feet slipped on the loose shale and stones sending them bouncing and rattling down the slope. Sucking in a deep breath, he tried to still the feeling of apprehension in him. They were making too much noise, that much was for sure. If Mannix had not spotted their approach across the desert, he must surely know of their presence among the rocks by now.

'Quiet,' he hissed savagely as the others clattered behind him. 'Do you want them to be lying in wait for us along the trail?'

They rounded a sharp bend in the trail, put their horses to the steep incline that stretched away ahead of them. Every shadow seemed to hide a dark shape with a gun lined up on his chest, every crag the hiding place for Mannix, the man he had sworn to kill.

'How far to this cabin you were talkin' about?' he asked in a harsh whisper.

The man rode up beside him, bending low in the saddle, pointing directly ahead of them. 'Not much further now, Mister Kearney. About a quarter of a mile around the bend there.'

'I guess that's the place they'll have

headed for,' muttered the other. He spoke calmly, trying to convince himself as much as the others. He wanted Mannix and those from the stage to be there, not wandering around in the rocks, ready to attack from any direction. Not that three men and three women could do much to stop the force he had at his back, he thought tightly. They might have time in which to get in one lucky shot, but that would be all. Once his men dropped into cover among the rocks, it would soon be the end for Mannix and any of the others who decided to throw in their lot with him.

Some ratlike flare of spirit returned to his mind at that thought and he held himself taut in the saddle, still gripping the sixshooter, ready to use it on anything that moved.

Ahead of them, the trail twisted up the face of the mountain slope, a dimly seen grey scar in the moonlight. Rounding the bend, he halted the men, holding up the hand which held the pistol, the barrel glinting brightly in the moonlight. They had only a little way to go now, he estimated, if the outlaw's memory had been true and he didn't want to go into this place with his eyes shut. He was debating whether to split his force in two and send one group over the rocks on foot, to attack the cabin from the rear when he heard the slight sound among the rocks to his right. Swiftly, he swivelled in his saddle, slitting his eyes against the moon as he searched the shadows intently, trying to pick out whatever it was that had made the sound.

For several moments, he could see nothing. The rocks were bare and still all about him. Had he imagined the sound? he wondered broodingly. This place was enough to make any man's imagination run riot with him. Too still, too quiet. A whole army of men could be hiding out there, close to the trail, and no one would be aware of it.

Then he caught a fragmentary glimpse of the shadow that moved swiftly at the very edge of his vision. He lifted his right hand, aimed the Colt quickly, and almost without thinking, snapped a couple of shots at the fleeing figure, running from shadow to concealing shadow in the moonlight, less than thirty feet away.

'There goes one of 'em!' he yelled at the stop of his voice. 'Shoot him down!'

He put spurs to his mount, felt the animal leap forward, feet clattering gratingly on the rocks. The man had vanished a moment earlier, and he felt certain that neither of his shots had hit their target. But the man was heading back in the direction of the cabin and if they hurried, they stood a chance of cutting him off, catching him like a jack rabbit out in the open where they could shoot him down at their leisure. His horse clambered over rough rocks, leapt forward. The next second, twin blasts of gunpowder erupted on either side of the track and he felt himself being hurled out of the saddle as his mount went down under him.

7

Rawhide Vengeance

Crouched down among the rocks, Cal heard the gunpowder blow, the twin explosions so close together that they sounded like one. The vivid orange-red flashes showed brilliantly in the dimness and as the last rumbling echoes died away, reflected from the rocky walls of the canyons, he heard the yells of wounded men and the shrill neighing of horses. Quickly, he slithered down a narrow funnel in the rocks, ignoring torn hands and knees. He hit the bottom with a jar that sent stabs of pain along both legs and up into his body. For a moment, he stood quite still, then ran over the rocks in the direction of the explosions. If he was to even up the odds a little, it was essential to work fast and hit the outlaws before they were able to collect their scattered wits.

He came out on a low ledge that overlooked the trail some twenty feet from where he and the other man had planted the two barrels of gunpowder. The blast had done its work well. He reckoned that more than half the bunch had been close enough to the gunpowder when it had gone off to catch most of the force of the blast. There were several bodies littering the rocky defile, unmoving humps of shadow. The others were still in the saddle, trying to quieten their rearing mounts. Narrowing his eyes, he tried to pick out Kearney, but there was no sign of the other. Either he had been killed by the blast, or he had taken to the rocks as soon as he realized what had happened, knowing that shots would soon come whistling among them from the rocks.

Carefully, Cal aimed at the men still milling around in the defile. Smoke still hung thickly over the scene, drifting away only slowly in the faint breeze. He let loose six shots that pitched four men from their saddles, their mounts cantering away down the trail in the direction of the cabin. At least, if they managed to fight off these outlaws, they would have enough horses to take them on to Red Rock.

A slug whined dangerously close to his head and he ducked back under cover with a muttered curse. At least one of the men had taken cover on the far side of the trail and he had not taken long in spotting him. Cautiously, he moved a few yards to one side, eased his body around a large boulder and peered out again. The men were urging their mounts back along the trail, fighting to quieten them. Terrified by the blast which had gone off almost under their noses, the animals were extremely difficult to control. Cal fired at one man as he tried to wheel his mount and ride back, saw the other stagger as the slug hit him. But the outlaw held grimly on to the reins, even though he was slumped sideways. Grimly, Cal sent another slug into him, felt a sense of satisfaction as the other pitched out of the saddle, hit the ground and rolled out of sight. The riderless horse continued on down the trail until it vanished from sight.

Dimly, he could hear a voice yelling orders from the far side of the trail, and a moment later, he recognized it as belonging to Kearney. The lawyer was calling the others to pull back and get under cover before they were all killed.

Another man spun out of the saddle before he could get under cover as Cal loosed a shot at him. Then there were no more targets. The others had slid from their saddles and dived into the rocks.

Lying back among the rocks, Cal breathed in powder fumes, swallowing thickly. The harsh, pungent stench hung in the still air all around him, vile and choking. With a surprised lift of his spirits, he realized that somehow, the odds had now been reduced to the point where they stood a good chance of defeating this bunch of killers. There could be no more than eight or nine of them among the rocks yonder, and some of them could have been injured by the explosions. Rocks and boulders had been hurled for several yards in all directions when those two barrels of gunpowder had burst.

The fire from the other side of the trail slackened now. The outlaws had drawn back among the rocks to regroup their force. They would be doing some thinking now, he reckoned. The trouble was that Kearney was still obviously alive. He was the driving force behind this attack. If he had been killed outright by the explosions, the others might have pulled out and ridden back into the desert when they realized that the battle was going against them. After all, this was really no fight of theirs. They merely robbed the stages and shot down the guards whenever they tried to prevent them. But to stand up against gunpowder was a very different proposition and one for which they really had no stomach. But no doubt Kearney would keep them together as long as he was alive. There was a sudden movement in the rocks at his back and he whirled swiftly, his finger tightening automatically on the trigger. Then he eased it off as a voice whispered. 'Hold your fire, it's me.'

The tall man edged his way forward, slithered sideways between a narrow cleft in the rocks, and knelt down beside him, peering forward into the moonlight.

'What's happening?' he asked hoarsely.

'They're holed up in the rocks yonder,' Cal whispered back. 'I figure that half of 'em were caught by the blast. I got four or five of 'em before they knew I was here, but there must be eight or nine of them still alive and kickin'. Kearney is with them, givin' the orders.'

The other nodded. 'We got four horses,' he murmured. 'They came riding right up to the cabin as large as life a few minutes ago. Reckon we can ride out of here if we can only take care of those *hombres* yonder.'

Cal nodded tightly. 'That ain't goin' to be so easy,' he muttered. 'They're well covered and we can't get across the trail to hit 'em from the rear without bein' seen ourselves. But the same holds for them. I don't reckon they'll try anythin' with real teeth to it from the front. Too exposed for their likin'. They prefer to surround a place and attack from all sides.'

'Sure, but how well do you know this place? What if they move further along that edge of the trail and then cut across open ground to the cabin, sneak in there while we're still here watching this stretch of trail?'

'That's possible,' Cal considered it carefully. Kearney was no fool. He would know by now that he was pinned down at this point and he would be scheming desperately in an attempt to find a way of regaining the initiative which he had lost so decisively when that gunpowder had gone off in his face. For a brief space, he peered across the trail, then nodded to the other. 'It's too goshdarned quiet, like you say,' he murmured. 'Let's get back to the cabin. We can be ready for 'em there and if they do try to rush the place, they'll have to expose themselves to our fire.'

Carefully, they edged back into the jumbled rocks. At the cabin, they found that the windows had been barricaded by the bits of furniture which had littered the cabin, so that there were spaces through which they could fire with almost complete immunity. Cal glanced around the place, then nodded, satisfied. 'I reckon we're ready for 'em now if they do decide to come,' he said softly. He motioned to the others to take up their positions at the windows. 'Open fire as soon as you see anything within range,' he said tersely, 'but make every shot count. We don't have any ammunition to waste.'

The girl came over and knelt beside him, the Winchester in her hands. Her face was a soft, pale blur in the dimness at his shoulder. 'We tied up the horses at the rear of the cabin,' she said quietly. Her voice was calm and even. 'They should be safe there until we're ready to use them.'

He smiled faintly. 'You seem sure that we're goin' to get out of this alive,' he said gently.

She nodded her head slowly. 'I am,' she declared with conviction. She opened her mouth to say something further, but it was never said for at that very moment, the sharp bark of a rifle echoed from the rocks in front of the cabin and a slug smacked against the wooden wall of the shack, embedding itself in the thick timber. The single shot seemed to be a signal, for as one the guns crashed in a wide arc around the narrow plateau, setting up a savage, echoing thunder in the stillness of the night. He made Norma crouch down still further as he sighted the Colts on the brief, stabbing flashes of light among the rocks, knowing that the heaviest attack would have to be a frontal one because of the lie of the terrain. He loosed off three shots into the darkness, saw a dark shape leap into the air behind one of the rocks and then bump down it to land in the open, with arms and legs outspread.

The girl lifted her head in spite of Cal's order for her to remain close to the floor. Out of the corner of his eye, he saw the small knot of men suddenly rush from cover and charge towards the door of the cabin. Swiftly, he aimed the Colt, squeezed the trigger. One shot blasted out, then the hammer fell on an empty cartridge. Cursing savagely, he tugged at the shells in his belt, knowing that there was little time in which to fill the chambers again and take proper aim. He could hear the thudding of the men's boots on the rocks outside as they ran towards the shack.

Instinctively, Norma lifted the rifle, thrust the tip of the barrel through the crack near the window and fired shot after shot into the knot of men. The gun went off with a series of staccato concussions that made the air in the room sing with their violence. Four of the running men collapsed as the slugs tore into them. They were caught out in the open and by the time Cal had stuffed shells into his Colts and lifted his head once more, there were only two left out of the knot of men, two men running back towards the rocks on the edge of the plateau. He shot them both down without compunction. Much as he disliked shooting men in the back, he knew that if they were to survive, they would have to finish Kearney's band of outlaws off as quickly as possible. Once he realized that the odds had been cut down to evens, he doubted if Kearney would remain around. He would realize that everything was against him and his only chance would be to ride hell for leather back to Sherman City and try to link up with the sheriff and the rest of the men he had sent back there. He was no coward, but he was also no fool. So long as he held a superiority in numbers, he would be content to try to fight them. But once that advantage was gone, he would pull out and wait for another opportunity to present itself.

To the side of the cabin, sixguns bucketed in a wild, uneven storm of lead. This time, the men kept themselves under cover as they fired. They had seen what had happened to their companions when they tried to rush the place; and they were not willing to take that same risk. Slugs beat a vicious tattoo against the walls of the shack or ricocheted with shrill wails of tortured metal into the night.

Unruffled, Cal continued to fire at the twinkling spits of light from the muzzles of the outlaw guns. It was easy to pick out the orange flashes in the shadows among the rocks. There were not so many of them now, possibly three or four. The other men lay in huddled heaps on the smooth plateau or among the rocks where they had been cut down. Five minutes later, the firing ceased. The outlaws had had enough for the time being. They had lost nearly the whole of their force and were getting nowhere.

'Hold your fire,' Cal called to the others. 'No point in wastin' ammunition. Reckon they've pulled back into the rocks to talk over their next move.'

'You think they may pull out and leave us alone?' murmured one of the men from the far window.

'It's possible,' Cal observed. 'They don't have many men left. Three or four, I reckon. Kearney must know that he doesn't stand a chance with so few men at his back and if he's got any sense he'll see that the play is goin' against him and his only chance is to ride hell for leather back into Sherman City and meet up with the rest of these killers, maybe get that attorney friend of his to try to get your stage line illegally, Norma.'

'But how can he do that?' she inquired anxiously.

'Can't say without knowin' a lot more about the law than I do,' Cal replied. 'Though I guess he could swear out that you were dead, killed by outlaws out here in the desert and say that he'd bought the line from you before the stage left for Red Rock. The crooked attorney friend of his would draw up the papers and witness 'em.'

'But all we would have to do is ride back into Sherman City to prove him wrong.'

Cal nodded. 'That's so I reckon. But by that time, he'll have taken over the line and he'll have more men at his back includin' the sheriff and the law in Sherman City, for what it is.'

'I see.' There was a dubious note to the girl's voice. 'I hadn't thought of that.'

They lay crouched behind the windows for several minutes, peering out into the darkness, striving to make out any sign of movement there, but there was nothing. The rocks seemed empty and deserted in the quiet moonlight and only the bodies of the men in the plateau gave testimony to the fact that the outlaws had been there at all.

Grunting a little, Cal got to his feet and moved cautiously to the door. Opening it a little, he peered out, listening intently for any sound. Far off, in the distance a coyote howled faintly, the dismal echoes sending little shivers running up and down his spine. He stood there for a while, then turned and looked back into the room. 'They could have pulled out,' he said shortly. 'I didn't hear their horses.'

'It could equally well be a trap,' warned one of the men. 'They may be out there now, waiting for us to step out into the open.'

That was true also, reflected Cal. He moved back inside. 'We'll wait until dawn,' he said quietly. 'If they haven't attacked by then, we'll get the horses and ride out.'

★ ★ ★

The night passed slowly. Sleep was out of the question for most of them, although the women dozed off intermittently. The air inside the shack was bitterly cold and they dared not light a fire. Cal was glad when the darkness began to fade a little and the first signs of an early dawn appeared low down in the east. The tumbled skyline of rock and boulder showed more clearly in silhouette against the heavens and the bright stars began to fade as the moon dropped lower into the west. Stretching to ease the cramp in his limbs, Cal got to his feet, peered out over the plateau. More and more, he was coming to the opinion that Kearney had decided that withdrawal was the better part of valour and that he had taken those men still alive with him and ridden out, leaving them to ride on into Red Rock. There were more important things for him to do now in Sherman City.

Slowly, Cal opened the creaking door of the shack. It swung back on twisted hinges. Drawing in a deep breath, he stepped out into the open. No shots came from the rocks overlooking the plateau and he breathed a little more easily. Going back into the hut, he shook the others awake.

'Time to move out,' he told them. 'Seems our friends have left during the night like we figured.'

'You sure?' asked the tall man, squinting up at him.

'Pretty certain,' Cal replied. 'But they may not have gone too far. The sooner we get out of here, the better.'

They rode out fifteen minutes later. Cal had the wounded agent over the saddle in front of him, and the others were mainly riding double. They would make slow time this way, but the outlaws had driven off the rest of the horses into the hills and finding them would have taken too much time. The journey through the rocks took them most of the morning and it was early afternoon before they rejoined the desert trail some miles to the north. The detour had taken them many miles from the main trail, more than Cal had thought. But now that he had got his bearings, he knew that long before nightfall, they would come within sight of the railroad and then the town of Red Rock.

At five o' clock, they were riding alongside the gleaming metal rails of the railroad and another thirty minutes saw them entering the outskirts of Red Rock. There were few people around on the dusty streets and the adobes seemed empty and quiet. The air still held a lot of the residual heat of the day and Cal guessed that most of the townsfolk were still at siesta.

'Reckon you had best ride on to the stage depot,' he said to the two men, 'and I'll take the agent to the doctor.'

'Will you come along to the depot?' asked Norma, eyeing him quietly.

He nodded, then gigged his mount along the main street, keeping a sharp look out for a doctor's place. He located one halfway along the street and hitched the horse to the rail outside then gently lifted the wounded man from the saddle, slung him over his shoulder and walked to the door of the office, knocking loudly on it.

For several moments, there was no sound inside the office, then he heard the shuffling of feet at the other side of the door and a second later it opened, to reveal a tall, thin-faced man, his grey hair shining a little in the sunlight. He gave Cal a quick glance that took in everything, then stood on one side and motioned him in.

'Move inside and set him down on the table through there,' ordered the other tersely. He followed Cal into the side room, went over to the far corner as the other laid the injured man on the long table. The doctor came over a moment later, began to peel the agent's shirt from his chest, then pulled off the bandage and the padding over the wound. His face was grave and serious as he saw the condition of it.

'We got caught in a sand storm out there in the desert,' Cal explained quickly. 'I figure some of the dust must have worked its way into it. Haw bad is he, doctor?'

'Pretty bad. I'm not sure whether I can do anything for him.' The other's voice was slow and grave. 'There's an infection here. The wound was evidently clean to begin with, but the sand had got into it as you say.' He went back into the other room, returned with a basin of hot water and a cloth, began to clean the wound up, wiping away the congealed blood around the edges. His lips were pursed tightly together as he worked, not once looking up. Then he said: 'This man is the stage agent from the way station, isn't he?'

'That's right. Outlaws attacked us while we were there, fired the barn and the station itself and spooked all of the horses. We had to make it out across the desert on foot.'

The doctor stared up at him in incredulous surprise. 'You crossed the desert on foot?' he said tightly.

'Seven of us, including him,' Cal

acknowledged. 'Miss Holmes who owns the stage line, and four passengers. The outlaws holed us up in a shack out in the rocks some fifteen miles from here. We managed to fight 'em off and collect four of their horses.'

The doctor stared at him inscrutably for a long moment, then he nodded slowly. 'That stage has been held up several times in the past few weeks. They've lost a few drivers too. It's getting way past a joke, but nobody seems to be able to do anything about it.'

'There's a sheriff in Red Rock, isn't there?' Cal asked. 'You reckon he might get a posse together and ride back with us to Sherman City?'

The doctor considered that for a moment and then shook his head slowly. 'I doubt it. Sherman City isn't in his territory. They have a sheriff there. If you reckon there's any need for the law at the other end of the line, you'd have to call on him.'

Grimly, Cal muttered: 'That's not possible, I'm afraid. You see, he's in cahoots with the outlaws. He warned them we were takin' the stage out of town yesterday morning and they were ready for us. He's been feedin' them the information which allows them to know when to attack the stage.'

'You sure of that?' Surprise was still in the doctor's tone. 'That's a pretty serious accusation to make, you know.'

Cal nodded. 'I know. But I've got the proof of it. Kearney, the lawyer in Sherman City is the leader of the gang. He led the men who tried to hunt us down and kill us in the desert.'

The other went back to attending to the wounded man, working skilfully as he cleaned the wound, then probed to make certain the slug was not still in the man's body, before sterilizing the wound and binding it up once more. When he had finished, he turned to Cal. 'I think you'd better leave him here with me for a while. I can put him up in the bed through yonder. If he has a strong constitution and plenty of luck, he'll pull through but it will be a long progress. Had you been able to get him to me right away, things would have been a whole lot easier, both for me and him.'

Grimly, Cal said: 'I reckon things would have been a whole lot easier on all of us, doctor.'

Outside, he climbed wearily into the saddle. There was a deep-seated tiredness in his limbs now and he could not remember when he had last slept properly. He seemed to have been awake for weeks since pulling out of Sherman City with the stage. He rode slowly along the street, switching his gaze from side to side until he located the stage depot where he had booked his ticket to Sherman City all those days before, seeking only to settle down in this country in peace.

Red Rock was an untidy town. The rough adobes were scattered about it in all directions, while in the centre, there were a couple of hotels, the sheriff's office and the stage depot dominating everything else. The railhead too stood a little distance from the depot, the gleaming rails running off into the desert in both directions. At the moment, the station was deserted and there was no sign of smoke as far as the eye could see. He deliberately put the weariness from him as he dismounted and went inside the depot to find the girl waiting for him. She gave him a glad smile as she came forward. Behind the desk, the clerk watched with a serious look on his long, sad features.

'How is he?' she asked quickly.

'The doc reckons he may have a chance. There's an infection and he's done all that he can for him at the moment, but it's goin' to be a long while before he's up and kickin' again, I'm afraid. The sand gettin' into the wound caused all the trouble, it seems.'

'I thought it would,' the girl nodded. She took his arm. 'Let's get something to eat and then we can plan what to do next.'

'We'll have to get the law with us whatever we do,' he said quietly, 'otherwise there's little we can do. If we ride back into Sherman City without men at our back we don't stand a chance. Kearney will have marshalled his men together now and he'll be expectin' us to ride back. He'll be ready for us.'

'Do you think we can trust the sheriff here?' asked the girl, as they walked out and over to the hotel.

'We've no other choice. There ought to be some honest men around.'

* * *

They went into the hotel and ordered a meal. The floor was covered with a thin film of sand and the waiter was a thin, sallow-faced man who seemed to carry a toothpick permanently between his lips, but the food proved to be far better than the place itself and they both ate ravenously as steak, potatoes and eggs were brought for them, finishing with black coffee, hot and strong. The waiter idly watched them eat, standing with his elbows propped against the door-way.

There were evidently few visitors in town at that time of the year and they were able to get a couple of rooms without any difficulty. Cal went into his and washed the grime and dust off his face, then put on a fresh shirt from his pack, feeling better. Down in the street, the shadows were beginning to stretch themselves out now that the sun was dipping swiftly towards the west. Meal time being over, there were several people in the street, most of them making their way over to the saloons. A few were gathered around the stage depot and he guessed that the news they had brought with them had spread through the town and some folk were interested in what had happened.

Downstairs, in the lobby, he waited for the girl to come down. When she appeared, he got up out of his chair and moved to meet her. 'Ready to have a word with the sheriff?' he asked.

She nodded. 'Let's get it over with,'

she said in a determined tone.

They stepped out on to the board-walk. The air was cooler now, and there was a slight breeze blowing along the street, kicking up little whirls of dust and carrying them along out of sight. The sheriff's office was thirty yards away on the other side of the street, the dusty window glinting a little in the last red rays of the setting sun. Cal rapped loudly, then pushed open the door and went inside.

The tall figure lying back in the chair behind the desk, his head sunk forward on his chest did not move as they walked forward. Cal eyed him curiously for a moment, then glanced across at the girl, a faint smile on his lips. Going forward, he paused in front of the desk, then brought the flat of his hand down sharply and loudly on the wood in front of the dozing man. The smack was like a pistol shot in the room.

The sheriff jerked upright as quickly as if a gun barrel had been thrust into the small of his back and blinked up at them, squinting against the light.

'What goes on?' he demanded harshly, licking his lips. He swung his legs to the floor and got unsteadily to his feet.

'Sorry to wake you like that,' murmured Cal softly, 'but what we have to tell you is important.'

Briefly, Cal outlined to the other what had happened, giving him the proof they had that not only was Scott Kearney the leader of the band of outlaws who had been attacking and robbing the stages through to Sherman City, but that the sheriff there was also in cahoots with them. When he had finished, the other stared up at him out of frosty eyes, then gave a brief nod. 'And you want me to swear in a bunch of deputies and ride out into Sherman City with you and try to put things to rights there, is that it?' he demanded.

'That's it in a nutshell,' Cal said.

The other shook his head. 'Afraid I can't do that, mister,' he said grimly. 'Not that I don't believe you. What you've told me may be true, or it may not be. That's no real concern of mine. All my duty is, is to keep law and order in Red Rock and the surrounding territory. I ain't got no authority at all in Sherman City. I can't get a posse together and ride out there to arrest the sheriff even if he is in cahoots with these outlaws as you claim.'

'You mean to say that you'll sit here and let them go scott free?'

'I've got no other choice. Only the Rangers or a United States Marshal could help you out in this case, I'm afraid.'

Cal sighed, his face grim and tight. 'So you refuse to do anythin' to help?'

'That's the way it is, mister. I'm sorry, but there ain't a thing I can do.' The other sank back into his chair, leaned back and regarded Cal evenly.

For a long moment, Cal stood there, facing the other, feeling the anger boil up inside him. He knew inwardly that what the other said was possibly true. The man's authority extended only so far and not further. It was the same as if a man had ridden south over the Mexican border. No one could touch him there. Anyone broke the law in Sherman City and only the law there would be able to deal with it, and if the man supposed to uphold the law was in the pay of Scott Kearney, then those outlaws were completely safe until the townsfolk threw the sheriff out and elected a straight-shooting man in his place. There wasn't much chance of that happening, he thought wearily.

He turned to the girl, shrugging his shoulders. 'Seems there's nothin' more we can do here, Norma,' he said harshly. 'Let's get out of this place. There's somethin' here I don't like.'

★ ★ ★

They went back to the hotel and up to their rooms. Standing by the window, staring down into the street, Cal felt defeat lie heavily on him. It seemed that Kearney had won out in the end after all. On the face of it, there was nothing he or the girl could do here. Nobody in town would ride back with them and give them support. And they could do little by themselves. Kearney or the sheriff would see to it that they were stopped long before they rode into Sherman City.

But there had to be a way, he thought fiercely. He was damned if he was going to give up this easy. How to get into Sherman City quickly and without being seen by any of Kearney's men along the trail?

In the distance, he heard a faint moaning wail and several seconds passed before he realized what it was; before he even realized that here was the answer to their problem. The railroad. It was the only way to get into Sherman City without using the trail. There was sure to be a train out sometime the next morning and if he and the girl were on it, they would reach Sherman City before nightfall the same day. He felt a fresh lift to his spirit. At the moment, he did not know what they could do once they did get into Sherman City, but that was a bridge they could cross once they reached it. It was possible that the girl had some friends there, someone she could turn to, who might help her. She had lived there for a long time, as long as Scott Kearney, and if they could rally enough support quickly enough before Kearney could do anything to combat it, then they might stand a chance.

* * *

The train drew out of Red Rock the next morning with a clanking of metal and a mighty hissing of steam, gathered speed slowly as it moved along the incline which led west into the desert. Seated by the window, Cat watched the stretching vastness which they had crossed in such discomfort only a few hours before, move smoothly past them. There were several other passengers on the train, but none of them paid him or the girl any attention.

Norma leaned forward in her seat, spoke softly under her breath. 'This plan of yours, Cal, do you think there's any chance? We seem to be taking an awful risk going back into Sherman City like this.'

'If any of your friends will help us, we may be able to act quickly enough to throw Kearney off balance. It's our only chance. If the law won't, or can't, help us, we have to do things this way. We have no other choice open to us.' He did not go on to say that, even if there were others in Sherman City, willing to back them against a man as powerful as Scott Kearney, their chances of success were remote indeed. Few men would be willing to go up against professional gunmen such as those who were backing Kearney, and with the law apparently on his side.

The train chugged its way over the desert, moving far more quickly than even the stage. This was certain to be the mode of travel in the years to come,

Cal reflected idly, leaning back in his seat and surrendering himself to the swaying motion of the train. He could visualise the time when a vast network of these steel tracks was laid over the length and breath of the whole country, stretching from New York clear to California in the west. But that time was still some years away and until it came, the stagelines would have their day and it was essential that they should not be allowed to fall into unscrupulous hands.

The day passed slowly. It was hot inside the train and dust and sand from the desert drifted continually in through the windows whenever they were opened to let in a little air. Shortly before nightfall, Cal caught his first glimpse of Sherman City in the distance as the train rounded a long, shallow curve. The sky was changing swiftly into a haze of red and gold as the sunset flared over the town. He felt the tension beginning to rise in him, over-riding every other emotion, now that the time of showdown was approaching fast. He saw the girl watching him closely, knew that the same kinds of thoughts were running through her mind at that moment.

The train began to slow as the brakes were applied with a screeching of metal on metal. Fifteen minutes later, they drew into the station at Sherman City. With a shrill hiss of steam, the engine came to a standstill. Cal got to his feet, looked down at the girl and forced a quick, grim smile. 'I guess it's time we looked up those friends of yours,' he said gravely.

She nodded, got to her feet and moved down the coach ahead of him, stepping out on to the platform. Several other passengers alighted and moved with them out into the main street.

'I reckon we'd better head for the depot,' he said quietly, glancing about him in the growing dimness.

They walked slowly along the boardwalk, keeping into the shadows. The town seemed quiet, but Cal could sense an undercurrent of something which prickled in his nerves and lifted the small hairs on the nape of his neck uncomfortably. It was as if they had come in at the tail end of a gun battle and the air had not yet quite cleared of gunsmoke. But that was imagination, of course, he told himself grimly. A group of horsemen rode around the corner, edged their mounts towards the stage depot and got down from their saddles.

Instinctively, Cal drew the girl back into the shadows, his fingers tightening on her arm. He had a dreadful instant as he eyed the men. Were they the sheriff and his outlaw band, riding openly into town now, utterly sure of themselves? A moment later, the girl uttered a sharp cry and in spite of his grip on her arm, tore herself free and ran forward across the road. For a moment he stood irresolute, not sure of what was happening, then stepped across to follow her. A group of the men came forward at her sudden cry, then she turned to him, with a faint look of wonder written on her face.

'This is Clem Bailey and some of his men,' she said quickly. 'They are old friends of the family, came here with my father many years ago.'

Cal felt his hand gripped strongly by the grey-haired man. 'We came here to force a showdown with Scott Kearney and the sheriff,' he said, trying to explain, but the other cut him off.

'Clem, your driver Norma, warned us what was happening when I went along to see him shortly after the stage had pulled out. We were waiting for the sheriff and his men when they tried to ride back into town. Most of 'em are in Boot Hill right now, and the others are in jail. Kearney came riding back yesterday but there was a welcomin' committee waitin' for him too. He's in jail with the others and I reckon there'll be a rope waitin' for him after the trial.'

He glanced round at the rest of the men with him, then gave a quick grin. 'Me and the boys are steppin' into the saloon,' he said quietly. 'But I reckon you'd like to take a walk and see Clem.'

Cal nodded, waited until the batwing doors had closed behind the men, then turned to the girl. There was peace in Sherman City now, he felt sure of that.

THE END

We do hope that you have enjoyed reading this large print book.

Did you know that all of our titles are available for purchase?

We publish a wide range of high quality large print books including:
**Romances, Mysteries, Classics
General Fiction
Non Fiction and Westerns**

Special interest titles available in large print are:
**The Little Oxford Dictionary
Music Book, Song Book
Hymn Book, Service Book**

Also available from us courtesy of Oxford University Press:
**Young Readers' Dictionary
(large print edition)
Young Readers' Thesaurus
(large print edition)**

For further information or a free brochure, please contact us at:
**Ulverscroft Large Print Books Ltd.,
The Green, Bradgate Road, Anstey,
Leicester, LE7 7FU, England.
Tel:** (00 44) **0116 236 4325**
Fax: (00 44) **0116 234 0205**

THE WIND WAGON

Troy Howard

Sheriff Al Corning was as tough as they came and with his four seasoned deputies he kept the peace in Laramie — at least until the squatters came. To fend off starvation, the settlers took some cattle off the cowmen, including Jonas Lefler. A hard, unforgiving man, Lefler retaliated with lynchings. Things got worse when one of the squatters revealed he was a former Texas lawman — and no mean shooter. Could Sheriff Corning prevent further bloodshed?

CABEL

Paul K. McAfee

Josh Cabel returned home from the Civil War to find his family all murdered by rioting members of Quantrill's band. The hunt for the killers led Josh to Colorado City where, after months of searching, he finally settled down to work on a ranch nearby. He saved the life of an Indian, who led him to a cache of weapons waiting for Sitting Bull's attack on the Whites. His involvement threw Cabel into grave danger. When the final confrontation came, who had the fastest — and deadlier — draw?

RIVERBOAT

Alan C. Porter

When Rufus Blake died he was found to be carrying a gold bar from a Confederate gold shipment that had disappeared twenty years before. This inspires Wes Hardiman and Ben Travis to swap horse and trail for a riverboat, the *River Queen*, on the Mississippi, in an effort to find the missing gold. Cord Duval is set on destroying the *River Queen* and he has the power and the gunmen to do it. Guns blaze as Hardiman and Travis attempt to unravel the mystery and stay alive.

BLACK RIVER

Adam Wright

John Dyer has come to the insignificant little town of Black River to destroy the last living reminder of his dark past. He has come to kill. Jack Hart is determined to stop him. Only he knows the terrible truth that has driven Dyer here, and he knows that only he can beat Dyer in a gunfight. Ex-lawman Brad Harris is after Dyer too — to avenge his family. The stage is set for madness, death and vengeance.